THE OLD HOUSE

AND

OTHER SHORT STORIES

THE OLD HOUSE

and

Other Short Stories

Isabel García Cintas

This is a work of fiction. Names, characters, places and incidents are the product of the author's imagination. Any similarity between living or dead people, or companies, businesses, events, institutions or places is a coincidence.

Published by Amancay Ediciones, USA
Author website: www.isabelgarciacintas.com
isabelgarciacintas@ymail.com

Pictures and layout design: I. Jakovljevic
Author Photograph: T. Jakovljevic
English Editing: Marina Corleto Friedman

First Edition

The Old House and Other Short Stories
ISBN 978-0-9838523-6-0
Copyright ©2019 / Isabel García Cintas

To Rosa Amanda

(The short story), ultimately so secret and self-contained, sea snail of the language, mysterious brother of poetry in another dimension of literary time.

Julio Cortázar (1914-1984)

The Old House

A few months ago I dreamed again of the old house. But this time it was daytime, the *siesta* sun was hitting the asphalt of the avenue, and even the shadows of the thick trees were sunlit. I opened the gate of the garden and entered hesitantly. I walked through the veranda and the rooms, to my favorite reading corner. The whole house was bathed in light. Satisfied, I retraced my steps slowly and deliberately out to the street. I closed the gate behind me saying goodbye forever.

And just like that, the house let me go.

Then I opened my eyes. My bedroom was dark. I read in the luminous letters of the alarm clock that it was three in the morning. Smiling, I turned over and continued to sleep, without images.

That was a remarkable dream, but the inexplicable part of it became clear only yesterday when I met my sister again. I want to put it on paper right now and then toss it into my mental drawer of forgotten things, where the old family stories rest. Those memories that unite us, but which we rarely mention. Those that escape our understanding.

How to explain what happened? I would not believe it myself if someone would tell me such a thing.

For many years, back in my twenties, I cultivated a repertoire of repetitive dreams. Before that, I had never dreamt much, so the recurrence provoked in me a certain curiosity.

During childhood and adolescence, I had enjoyed a sound, deep sleep: I rarely dreamed anything. In my family though, dreams, particularly those announcing events that were yet to happen, were frequent and taken seriously, so I felt I should ignore the subject. Born in the last half of the twentieth century, I considered myself a woman of the times. So premonitions, to me, were just not credible.

Years later, when they started, the dreams took me far away. Some of them to a nocturnal world with places unknown to me, but which eventually became familiar, meticulously detailed spaces. They were not dreams that stood out for their thematic elements, no. Those repetitive dreams were like slivers of more complete stories that I could only glimpse for a moment, like when we read an excerpt of a book in a newspaper article, or we notice, in the shrewdly truncated scenes of a preview, how exciting the movie coming out will be.

Among the many curious and unknown nocturnal sites I visited in my dreams during those two decades, I remember the large movie hall well. These dreams were frequent, and they frustrated me. The theater was particularly interesting because when I sat down, the seats faced anywhere but the screen. I tried many times to enter the theater a different way, through other doors. I even climbed a staircase behind curtains and sat on the mezzanine. However, I never got to see the movie in front of me.

But the old house was not just a dream, the old house existed (and perhaps still does). There, my sister and I spent our adolescence. With Mom and Dad, we lived happy and sad moments, like every other family. In that house, we had a healthy family life without significant setbacks, except for the routine of minding the budget to make it to the end of the month. So, why such dark dreams? Always at nigh time I would be walking towards the door, or already inside, or leaving, but with anguish in my chest, feeling the urgency to leave and, somehow, with the fear of not being able to do it. Luckily, I always left the house, but anxious, with a sense of imminence that something was about to happen to me.

Although vague at the beginning, the dreams ended up annoying me because they were repetitive. There was lingering anguish after waking up, as it happens with some nightmares. Years passed, and I always wondered what they meant, if they had any meaning at all.

Then, one day, while flipping through a magazine in the dentist's waiting room, the kind I wouldn't buy because they have too many advertisements and little content, I found an article about recurring dreams. I was surprised since it was the first time I had seen something writtcn on this subject. I read it with interest and decided to put the advice into practice. After all, what could I lose? At least I would have tried something.

I prepared mentally for it, but without much hope. One night, shortly after, the dream reappeared. The weird thing is that, while being in it, I remembered the advice I had read in the magazine and decided to act. It was effortless. I stopped at the front door and said to the house, or to the dream, or to myself, who knows: "Now I will leave here, I will cross the garden, I will close the gate, and I will leave. Forever. I do not want to come back, and I do not want this dream, never again." And I left, nervous, walking down the empty avenue right in the middle where it was not so dark, and I kept walking until I woke up.

The dream disappeared for a while. Then suddenly one night, I returned to the house. That was a few months ago. And it was daylight. I was not the same dream. The house and I had made peace.

When I met my sister again, I told her what had happened with satisfaction and still some disbelief. "Even if it sounds weird to you, that's how I got free from that dark dream, acting on it voluntarily. Sounds unbelievable, doesn't it?"

I had never told her about my dream before. Our international telephone talks had always been brief and to the point, with other pressing issues to address. She fixed her eyes on mine, wide with surprise. There was a silence as if she could not find the words, and I looked at her questioningly.

"Twice unbelievable, or better, triple," she said, at last, her voice a little strangled with emotion. "I had the same dark dreams with the movie theater and the old house for years! They were quite unpleasant, but one day the fear and the darkness disappeared. Then suddenly, not long ago, I dreamed of the house again but as I remember it, bathed in sunlight."

She paused as I tried to understand what she was saying, our eyes unflinching, connected by an invisible thread of surprise that united us beyond words.

Rosita sighed, still amazed. "It seems you took me out with you when you left the house and closed that door."

We looked at each other for some time, saying nothing.

"Let's get the kettle going for some tea," was all I could muster. She nodded, her eyes damp with tears and we walked slowly toward the kitchen.

Editor's Note: This story won Third Prize at the literary contest 2007 Las Américas, organized by the Miami Dade College.

Lunch at Chez Antoine

María Laura

Still, three hours to go. Time enough. I better takc a shower once and for all. Or better, not yet. I am so nervous that I'm sure I'll get all sweaty gain before getting dressed to go. Okay, calm down. What did Carola say I had to do? Breathe deeply, loosen up and remember that I am not the only one who is nervous. To concentrate on the fact that I have wanted this all my life, blah, blah. But the truth is that when thinking about it... all those years, on so many sleepless nights... I never expected I would tremble like this, and I'm still not even out of the door. I don't know what to wear yet, for goodness sake! You still have more than two hours to go, Laurita, calm down. Wait. Again, I called myself Laurita. I do not know where that comes from. Who knows what name they would have given me. Did they even think of a name? I didn't dare ask them. Coward. So many things I never dared to ask. Carola says it's okay, that I have to do it when I am ready and in a natural way. But there is nothing natural about this since I just told Mom and Dad that I was going to see my parents. But what do I wear? I do not want to go in jeans. If Mom were not so sad, I would call and ask her. But I can't, I don't want to burden her with this silliness of my wardrobe doubts too. I already hurt them enough. Poor dears. They were wrecked but managed to smile, so as not to disappoint me. Because I saw clearly in their eyes what they felt when I told them I was going to meet them. To meet the others. What a mighty mess. Who are the others here? My birth parents, or Mom and Dad? I call them "my parents," and Carola said it's okay. They are my parents, because "Mom and Dad" will always be that to me. But Carola is snug in her office while I am the one who has to be here, to put my face, body, and soul in the hands of those strangers who probably did not even knew they were conceiving me! Who knows where or how. Did they even reach orgasm? Both of them? Or am I the result of some casual and trivial encounter? Will I ever find out? OK, I can't believe I'm having these thoughts. I don't even know them. Will they like me? That's what worries me. I think I'm afraid of being judged, not accepted. But Carola said that this fear is normal, so cut it out and don't panic, Laurita. Stop procrastinating and get into the shower!

Marisa

This time Gino gave me a good haircut, and the color looks natural too. I'm glad because it doesn't always end up this way. I want to look elegant and endearing for her. And for Ricardo also, after all these years. A quarter of a century without seeing him. He did not send me any pictures, and neither did I. The one I emailed to her was the best I had on hand. She's so pretty! What would she think of me?

She was looking for us. My babe. I call her "my babe." So many years of thinking, of feeling her that way. Of not allowing myself to give her an identity other than the one I felt when I saw her for the first and last time. When she stopped crying and looked at me, although I knew she still could not see me, I felt those eyes piercing me to the bottom of my soul. As if she knew, as if she asked me why? I had relived those few minutes so many times in my mind. The nuns only allowed me to cradle her for a brief moment, but not long enough. "Don't get used to her," they said. What would they know? How can one not become familiar to a part of oneself that will be there forever and cannot be separated, even if it is taken far away? It is always in there, and that is definitive. At some point, I even thought that it would have been better not to have had her. Maybe it would have been better to have committed a mortal sin to avoid the guilt I've lived with. Maybe I would have been able to live another life, like the rest of the women around me. Now, after so many years and so many lies, came the call I never expected. As soon as I heard his voice I knew that, although we did not know each other much, Ricardo also carried the memory of our baby and the pain of letting her go. How childish... how ignorant we were. If only we had known how difficult it was going to be. "Live is full of unexpected turns," as Aunt Cata used to say. To think that he, an athlete, incredibly handsome, spent all that weekend with me. Me, an unattractive skinny girl. How could we have known then that that weekend was going to mark us forever? Now he wants to see me, and I want to see him too. We are bound by that weekend and by the guilt of giving away our baby, of losing her forever. She will never forgive us. I'm sure. And how to explain, if she asks us for explanations? Ricardo trusts that if she has sought us it is because she wants to know, nothing more, that she must also have her fears and doubts. Is he still as handsome as he was then? What an idiotic thought! I better get dressed and leave on time. I still have to get a taxi. I do not feel the strength to take the subway. Where did I put the restaurant's address? Ah, yes, here. *Chez Antoine*. How should I pronounce it? Ricardo said it is a French bistro, very discreet. He sounded like a worldly man on the phone. Let's see, one last look. I'm shaking from top to bottom. Get a grip of yourself! OK. Again, take a deep breath.

Ricardo

I hate when I get so nervous before a meeting. I usually stay calm so I can negotiate well. Dad taught me that. He got me to stop toying with sports and work hard at math. The old man was right, after all. If not, where would I be now? But today I'm anxious, impatient, and I can't focus. At least Marisa sounded calm and coherent. That little blonde from school. One of the most serious and the least flirtatious, who would have thought she'd be so good in bed? A total surprise. Tough luck I was already hooked up with Silvia and her family, and the scholarship her old man's acquaintances helped me get. Marisa did not stand a chance. Poor Marisa. She endured the worst, and she had to do it on her own: the troubles it caused with her parents and then the long months in that clinic for single pregnant girls to hide her belly. The baby had to go, and although I was not allowed to even see her, I'm sure she was beautiful. Fuck! My stomach still wrenches when I think of them there, alone in that place. I stood at the door, begging that nun to allow me just five minutes with them. I wasn't in love with Marisa, of course. It was something raw, coming straight from my gut, a strange thing that I have never felt again. I really don't like stirring these memories now, but I started this mess. I thought it would be easier though. Things always turned out to be easy for me. Except with Silvia, that lunatic, who left me for another man. An artist, at that. But all the better, because by that time we couldn't stand the sight of each other. Still, I was shaken for years. And suddenly, as if falling from the sky, Marisa's name appeared on that list of professionals. Marisa Cardozo. Single? "Yes, I never got married." Her voice trembled, but she chuckled to hide it. And the emails, what a delight. Mature and sensible, with a touch of humor. Who would have thought? Unbelievable how many things we agreed on. So, I dared to suggest the idea of looking around for the baby. By now a twenty-five year old woman. And she caught on. And even more amazing, the baby, Maria Laura is her name, was herself looking for us too. Is there such a thing as the transmission of thoughts? No, of course not, what am I saying. I wonder how Marisa's life might have been? She sounded youthful. Now, let me see these abs. OK, pretty flat, so far. And the biceps, not bad for an almost forty-six year old. Marisa liked the idea of a quaint French bistro. They know me well there, so I asked for that table in the corner, the most discreet. Now, if my hands would stop shaking, I could shave. Those two women are the closest thing to a family I have left. But, what if it doesn't work? Enough! Stop worrying. It has to work.

Editor's Note: This story won Second Place in the contest Poets and Narrators of 2012 organized by the Instituto de Cultura Peruana of Miami and the magazine Mujer, and featured in the Anthology published that same year by the I.C.P.

A Cry for Help

I look out the window at the drizzle while listening to Joan Manuel Serrat singing in his twenty-year-old voice: *It rains / behind the crystals / it rains and rains / over the half-leafless poplars / over the brown roofs / over the fields, it rains...*

But, of course, because I am in Florida there are no leafless poplars but tropical plants of luscious green that stand grateful, under the warm raindrops. Neither are there any brown clay roofs. Mercifully, I am surrounded by assorted plants with bright leaves that twinkle in the gray afternoon light. The only sort of brownish thing around here is the metal siding of the mobile homes in this trailer park where we ended up. This is the place where Pablo and I landed after we were laid off from that Miami Beach hotel. Pablo mows the lawns of the gringos' homes in Hollywood when it doesn't rain, and I clean by the hour inside those same houses, rain or no rain. Now I go back to listen to the music. This guy, Joan Manuel, always melts me. I'm a romantic, what can I say?

"A call for you. It's Tota. She seems to have gotten herself into another mess," says Pablo, cutting short my thoughts and handing me the cell phone, which luckily we can still pay to get in touch with the world.

"Tota," I say, lowering the volume of the music and getting ready to hear a long story, as usual. "What's up?" "I'm very worried, Piru, you have to help me get out of here," says Tota in a low voice, broken up by sobs. Again. She has been crying all the time since she got entangled with Antonio. At times, he is good-humored with his charming Central American accent, but he is definitely a bad guy. "Take it easy," I say, trying to calm her down. "What happened, tell me, I'm sure it was that jerk." "Ay, Piru, why didn't I listen when you told me that he was not what he seemed to be..." "Well, now it's a bit late for that, isn't it? What happened now? Are you by yourself there?" "Yeah, and the battery of the phone is running low. Listen, he's coming back at any moment now, and I have to hang up. I already packed my things. Please, come pick me up. Tonight I'm leaving him. I cannot stand him any longer. He gave me a black eye when I, by mistake, opened a drawer where he had stored a bunch of packages. He found me picking one up to see what it was." "And, what was it?" "I don't know, Piru, I didn't have time to see it. As soon as he saw me, he came to the door and knocked me out against the wall." "Son of a bitch! You have to leave him, Tota. Who knows what crap he has there. What did the packages look like?" "I think they were what we both think they were, but I'm not sure." Changing the subject, Tota pleaded: "Listen, I'm living him tonight, but now I'm afraid he'll be back soon... Would you please pick me up at the Shell station, after eight o'clock tonight?"

I look outside. It's pouring. I picture the Shell gas station, just across the freeway, a block from Antonio's trailer. I know it well.

"Sure, but be careful, don't let him see you. He'll hit you again." "No, I won't. He has to be somewhere else at seven-thirty; I overheard him on the phone. I am ready. Don't let me down." We pause, and for a second her melodic accent from Córdoba lingers in my ears. I reassure her. "Of course I'll be there, how couldn't I? Be careful, please. I will be parked right behind the Seven Eleven, so that nobody will see me, as always," I say with resignation, realizing I will miss an episode of Xica Da Silva, my favorite soap opera. I haven't missed one yet. "Thank you, Piru, I owe you another one. But I will not bother you guys this time. You can drop me off at any motel. He doesn't know where you moved so he won't be able to find me." "It's okay. We'll see about that later. Now you pretend that nothing is wrong so that he doesn't suspect. That son of a filthy bitch," I say. Then she adds, with a broken voice, "I don't know what I'd do without you, Piru..." "Shh, don't worry, that's what friends are for, right?" I say, with a bit of guilt, because I'm thinking that she's an idiot who couldn't foresee disaster even if it were a train that was coming right at her. I hang up with a grunt. Pablo looks at me with a smirk while handing me another mate.

"Tota knows how to wrap you around her pinkie... a few crocodile tears always do the trick. She looks for these rotten types, you know, thugs and bullies all of them." "I know, I know, but we grew up together. It's as if she were my sister. A sister who does not learn, of course! But she's the only person I have nearby from back home," I say as I sit and break down because this crappy afternoon has already turned out to be too emotional for me. The rain,

Joan Manuel's voice, and Tota again on my back. Like so many times since she left Córdoba in a rush, and I had the bright idea to invite her to share my room at the women's hostel on Avenida de Mayo. I was living happily in Buenos Aires since I had realized that if I stayed in the village, I would get old and die without seeing nothing of the world. But I always felt responsible for Tota, endlessly in so much need of a friend and guidance.

I savor the deliciously familiar taste of mate tea, and I realize that in this foreign place, what keeps me out of an asylum are Pablo, Tota, and yerba mate. And it's OK because it is not them who depend on me. I am linked to them by a familiar thread, a thread thousands of miles long that leads to the leafless poplars and the gray-tiled houses of my home town, hidden among Cordoba's cornfields. I give the mate back to Pablo and plant a kiss on his lips that he warmly returns.

I blow my nose and dry my tears again, looking out of the same window as the day Tota called. Pablo comes over and puts his kind, strong arm around my shoulders. Today is sunny, and the bright leaves of the palm trees shine against the summer sky.

It was a Saturday afternoon just like this, except it was raining. Then that night, it was still pouring when I drove slowly down the back alley of the Shell station. The lights of my car lit up the sides of the garbage cans, where so many times I had sneaked to meet Tota to pass her a few dollars. Because that scumbag Antonio would beat her if she did not take home the amount he expected after making her strut down the avenue in those platform heels. Poor Tota. And then I saw her, lying in a puddle of oily water, her neck twisted, her eyes open with fear, her clothes clinging to her stiff body and a few steps beyond, her drenched bag.

I shudder from head to toe, and he strokes my arm tenderly. I lean on his shoulder and cry until I calm myself for a while.

Editor's Note: This story was one of the three finalists at the First Cuentomania Contest, sponsored in 2015 by Miami Beach's Betsy Hotel, at the independent bookstore Books & Books of Miami.

Memories of a
Porcelain Doll

This morning they woke me up again. When the box opened and I could see, for a while it was hard for me to get used to the intense light, but I was happy to wake up. I don't mind the long intervals between each generation of the family when they put me to sleep, although nothing is better than to return. To be admired again, held and caressed and be part of the stories that the family girls create and recreate in their play. To witness their sadness and joys, watch them grow, and then let them go.

This morning my last mom opened the box in which she had put me to sleep many years ago. She carefully removed the pieces of tissue paper, until I finally was freed and exposed to the light of day. When she lifted me, my eyes opened. And, as it always happens when I wake up from my long slumbers, I found myself in an unknown room, in a house that I have never seen before.

"Hi," I thought, and wished I could smile, but I think she read in my eyes the affection with which I received the caress of her hand on my cheek. She is now a woman. The last time we met, she had turned eighteen and said farewell with misty eyes. When she cradled me goodbye in her arms, she had finished packing her books to go to college. Then she left me at her mother's home, another old mom of mine, inside the beautiful white box she had opened again with loving care today. This time she was accompanied by a little girl with familiar features.

"This is Sabrina," she said proudly, to her daughter. "Oh, Mom, she's beautiful!" "I told you, she was my favorite doll. From now on it is yours. You're going to take good care of her." The little girl took me in her arms, stroked me, and they both took off my clothes, leaving me with the soft, long linen camisole that covers my porcelain body. They took the light green dress with white ribbons to wash and iron, a ritual that leaves my dress neat and me looking most elegant. The silk skirt without wrinkles gracefully reaches down to my white sheepskin booties. I only mention this because I have actually checked myself in the mirror more than once. I look gorgeous, with my natural auburn curls falling on my shoulders and the bright, brown eyes with long lashes that open or close depending on whether I'm standing or lying down. I remember the artist who put the finishing touches on my little face long, long ago. He was young and handsome, and when he finished the last stroke he looked at me, his work or art, with great pride.

I'm sitting on my new mom's bed, looking towards the blue sky. The air is crystalline and fresh; outside there are golden, reddish leaves. A palette of colors is visible through the framed window with pink voile curtains. I see my new mom likes pink, as did her mom and her great-great-aunts. Pink brings back many memories.

Pale pink was the tissue paper they wrapped me in the first time they took me out of the display case where I was sitting, along with other dolls and toys, at that little gas lamp lit business many, many years ago. My first mother saw me through the window when she passed by, walking hand in hand with her father. I was wearing a blue dress with white bows, and it was right before Christmas Day on a busy street in Almeria, Spain. She looked at me for a long time, her little nose stuck against the glass. I remember her happiness when that Christmas Eve she opened the box and held me in her arms. "Her name will be Sabrina," she announced as she cradled me tenderly. Then she grew up and kept me in a box sleeping for a few years while she was busy in Cartagena getting married and raising her children, Francisco and María. When it was time to wake up, I found myself in María's arms, climbing aboard a large steam-boat on our way to Buenos Aires.

We lived in a couple of simple rooms in an immigrant's pension near the La Boca neighborhood, where people spoke a strange language; I heard it was Italian. Then we moved to different houses. Amanda was born, and when the family relocated to Cordoba, Maria had already grown up, and Amanda took me under her sole care.

So pink brings back memories. Pink was the dress Amanda wore the day she and her mother got off the tram and walked a block toward the house. I was comfortably snug on Amanda's left arm, her right hand in her mother's. That's when I heard the small explosions, three of them in a row. Amanda squeezed me trying unsuccessfully to hold her mother with the other hand, while she fell on her knees before laying, quiet, on the damp street. People ran, and I heard many screams, among them the desperate voice of Amanda calling her mother. I saw no more as she crushed me against her chest.

We ran together; we desperately ran because the person who fired the gun did not care that a woman, walking with her child, received the bullets meant for people standing on the opposite side of the street. We knocked on doors, terrified until someone sheltered us. I remember the pink dress with blood stains, like bright flowers on the pale linen, while Amanda, crying desperately, tried to answer the questions of a uniformed gentleman.

I did not see my first mom again. The last thing I remember was her limp body on the cobblestones. I was Amanda's companion and confidant for many years. I witnessed her tears and comforted her from the pain of having lost her mother, and the incurable wound of having seen her die like that. Years passed, and Amanda and Maria's brother, Francisco, got married and had two girls, while I slept in my box at Amanda's home.

When his older daughter needed a special doll to cradle in a kindergarten performance, Amanda sewed me a new green dress, and under Maria's nostalgic gaze, they gave me to her with tenderness. Then, my new mom grew up, she left the house to go away to college, and I slept soundly in my box again at her parents' house. Finally, one day she returned, took me with her and introduced me to her daughter in a beautiful city with lakes and mountains in Patagonia.

I traveled a lot with my new mom and saw many beautiful places. Then we moved here, far away, to the northern continent, near a huge lake called Erie. When her pink years passed, it was time for me to rest again, and I bid her farewell when she left for college.

Now I will go with my new mom throughout her childhood. I hear her speak in a different language, which I still do not understand. But I know that I will learn it soon. It's a beautiful autumn morning. As I was saying,... I can see the yellow-orange leaves glow in the morning air. As soon as I get my dress washed and ironed again, we will surely go out for a walk to explore this new city.

Slow Traffic

It happened on Biscayne Boulevard during the massive street renovation back in 2007. It was a Monday, one of the many loathed mornings rush hours of detours and rows and rows of slow moving of cars and trucks and buses wedged in line amid the noise of bulldozers and the loose, floating dust from the excavations lifted by the wind.

I was running late that day, and I was cursing the lack of environmental controls in Miami, looking at the exhaust smoke coming out of a passenger bus in front of me. I was inching patiently waiting to get to the next corner to find a way to any other street that would take me downtown.

Then I noticed the girl. She was walking anxiously back and forth between the door of a motel and the corner, just a few feet from my car. She was one of those provocative young women who occasionally worked through some areas of the boulevard, a picturesque remnant of what used to be a thriving business district in that neighborhood. New constructions, strict police rounds, and building improvements had already led to the remodeling of the old motels that, perhaps, still today harbor furtive transactions.

I never had to pay to be with a woman, but I liked to wink at them, or wave passing greetings. They worked from early morning strolling the boulevard until late at night, offering their bodies behind a heavy makeup and a skimpy wardrobe.

How ironic. They were walking outdoors while I was rushing to get into a cubicle with my name on it, on a floor of identical desks, with no access to windows, and unforgiving fluorescent lights, nine hours a day.

The bus in front of me stopped to load passengers. I braked and looked in the rearview mirror. Behind me, I could see the driver of a giant SUV make an annoyed face. I turned my attention to the girl just as a man rushed toward her and stood in front of her. Very close. He was young, muscular and tall.

Suddenly the guy grabbed her by the arm, she struggled to get free, and he slapped her, making her sway. I winced in my seat. She recovered, deftly freed herself from his grip and ran. She crossed in front of my car steady now on her high stilettos, the naked teenage legs under the miniskirt that with her running went high; the chest bouncing under her revealing neckline. I turned to the man. He had followed her a few steps, up to the sidewalk's curve. Alarmed, I looked back at the girl who, scurrying and stepping on puddles of water, reached the lane of the avenue where cars were coming from the opposite direction at a regular speed. In that split second, the thought that if she got run over none of us watching would be able to help her crossed my mind.

But she reached the sidewalk unharmed after dodging a truck. The tall guy again made a move to follow her, but he turned around cursing. The girl, always running, pulled out something that looked like a cell phone from her purse. The man made a sign to another guy not far away who crossed in front of the bus slowly avoiding cars, without losing sight of the runaway girl. He seemed ready to pursue whatever the other guy couldn't do.

All this happened in a matter of seconds, but I couldn't watch any longer because the SUV startled me with an irritated honk; the bus in front of me had already advanced quite a few yards, and we were moving again.

I pressed the gas and followed the line.

The Salt Storm

Matías adjusted the small backpack on his shoulder, picked up his sunglasses, locked the room and went down the hotel stairs. At the reception desk, he handed his keys to the concierge.

"Dinner is from eight to eleven p.m.," she said.

"Thanks," he answered, before walking out into the burning sun.

His classmates from the university had not yet reached the small town of Miramar, but since he had two days off before starting the project, he decided to take advantage of them. The heat in the plains by Mar Chiquita Lagoon hadn't diminished since before noon when he got off the bus. But the sweltering heat did not bother him after those recent fieldwork incursions to the mountains, where he felt the sharp cold cutting his bones.

The beach was, as he expected, busy with tourists who alternated between the thermal mineral baths, dips in the heavy salty waters and the temporary relief of the umbrellas. Flocks of birds often crossed the area in a concert of batting wings, cackling and bright colors that attracted attention, fascinated the children and motivated amateur photographers.

Matías walked for some time looking for a more secluded spot, and then he laid under the hot sun which reflected on the sand from the blue-white noon sky.

He mentally enumerated the steps that he was going to follow with his working group to survey the state of the waters and the flow of the tributary of the small sea, or Mar Chiquita. However, with the stillness of the afternoon, his recent lunch and mounting fatigue, he fell into a light, pleasant slumber.

Suddenly, he felt someone reclining at his side. When he opened his eyes, he found a beautiful face, framed by long chestnut hair, and a deep green gaze that looked at him intently. Still drowsy, he sat up halfway, and she backed up slightly, still smiling. A shudder ran through him, and Matías rubbed his eyes with both hands.

"Yes?" He asked, still a little sleepy, expecting she would say something.

But the woman was not there any longer. He looked around, now fully awake, and noticed that almost all the tourists had left the beach and the closest ones were several yards away. It was evident that he had slept for some time.

He rested his head on the towel again, wondering about the image he had just seen. Where did she go? Was it a dream? Then he thought that with the intense heat, he might have had a heat stroke, and if so, the girl Matías thought he had seen had only been a mirage. He decided to seek some shade and found a small outdoor bar under the trees. Looking around, with the odd feeling that he may actually find her, he ordered a fruit juice. He did not understand why he felt so uneasy. Surely it had been a dream prompted by the intense heat, which he had clearly underestimated. At a mirror behind the bar, he noticed that the sun had reddened his skin, and his hair seemed even lighter in contrast. He finally made his way to the hotel for an early dinner, still frustrated by the indefinable feeling left by his strange experience.

He crossed the streets of the small commercial downtown, full of tourists at dusk. He went through a bookstore without much interest, and in one of the regional craft shops, his sight fell on a table with figurines for sale. One of them caught his attention. He picked it up, bewildered. It was a slender woman chiseled out of wood, about eight or nine inches tall. Matías stared at her face, her memorable features and her hair falling on her shoulders.

I must be going crazy! It has to be the excessive sun, he told himself. The face of the statuette looked remarkably like the woman he saw on the beach. He examined it for some time, finding details that he had not noticed before; the rounded small bust, the slender waist and the skirt that fell on the perfect curve of her hips to reach the legs that ended in two delicate, bare feet, resting on a ceramic platform. The model must have been a woman much like the hallucination I had this afternoon, he told himself. So, yes, there was a real woman and, perhaps, she was the one he had seen on the beach. He wanted to believe that it was real. And he told himself again that he had possibly been out of it because of the heat and that's why it had seemed like a mirage. It was evident now that she existed; he had not dreamed of her. The thought filled him with expectations.

"How much?" He asked the busy cashier, holding the statuette in his hand.

"Thirty pesos," the girl replied.

Matías took the money out of his pocket and paid, enthralled by his acquisition. After the girl wrapped it in tissue paper, he walked out with the bundle in his hand, feeling an urgent need to open it and look at it again to verify that the model was indeed the girl on the beach and that he was not crazy.

When he got to his room, he placed the statuette on the nightstand. The figure looked to one side, as to something distant, the head high and the neck long and perfect down to its breasts. He turned it around, but still, the gesture was distant. Matías admired the skill of the artist, capable of carving a face so natural, almost as if painted on a canvas.

He checked his messages and then took a bath. While getting dressed, he glanced at the statuette every now and then. Finally, he went down to the dining room trying to escape the ridiculous spell of a wooden figurine. That's all it is, he told himself; a beautiful carved wooden figurine that, as a result of my sunstroke, is messing with my head.

In the dining room, he found two colleagues from the university who had gotten to town after him and joined them for dinner. They all agreed to go for a jeep tour along the coast of the lagoon the next day, to a famous abandoned European hotel built by German companies before the end of World War II. It was said in town that it had been built to welcome and hide European war fugitives and that the hotel was only open for a few years in the early 1950s. Then it was abandoned, and it stood on the coast, empty. The building looked too imposing for the small town, feeding legends of ghosts and international plots, stories undoubtedly fostered by tour operators.

The next day it was windy. He met his colleagues and walked toward the pier, but by noon the air was so contaminated with the salt that rose from the coast, that their eyes stung and their noses burned. The travel agency postponed the tour, so they returned to the hotel to wait until the wind subsided. In the street, pedestrians hurried to take refuge, and the reception and bar at the hotel were already full of frustrated vacationers.

"Another salt storm has come upon us," said the receptionist, with the confidence of a local who knows what is going to happen, and without flinching as the group of tourists from Buenos Aires bombarded her with questions, exasperated by the interruption of their thermal baths. "The storm has its cycle, so arm yourself with patience."

"It will be two days of loss, at least," said one of Matías' companions, studying his cell phone. "The long-distance buses scheduled to arrive will be temporarily suspended."

They looked at each other with concern. It would delay their job for the project on fresh waters and the management of the Rio Dulce's flow, which they hoped to present to the Senate Environmental Commission next month in Buenos Aires.

After lunch, the three met to compile data and organize papers. Two hours later they had finished, and Matías was left alone in the hotel bar, looking out the window at the deserted street. He was again thinking about his experience the previous day; he could not help ruminating on it over and over as if something were missing, although without a clue as to why or how this was happening.

Outside the wind swirled a salt powder that resembled fine snow. Matías imagined the whirlwind that would be rising upwards, in a spiral, slowly forming a salt plume. He had studied the phenomenon many times in NASA photos. It was similar to a hurricane in its form and the salt would cover the area.

He ordered a coffee and tried to concentrate on his paperwork. Suddenly he felt the eerie presence of someone by his side again. With surprise, he recognized the beautiful woman of his dream; the model of the statuette. A tremor ran from his head to his toes. He hesitated a few seconds, and she smiled at him with her sensual lips again, just like on the beach. He stood up.

"Can I join you for a moment?" She asked with an indiscernible accent.

"Of course," he said, surprised, adjusting the chair.

There was a long, embarrassing silence as she sat, crossing her slender legs. Matías turned his attention to the face of this beautiful stranger as conflicting thoughts crossed his mind. It was obvious that she was the model of the statuette, but he did not understand why she was there.

"I've surprised you! That was not my intention," she said in a cheerful tone, with a musical voice. "My name is Mampa Anzenuza."

"Matías Lamberti," he said, trying to compose himself and looking at her enthralled, "It's a pleasure."

Her dark green eyes, like the waters of the lagoon, studied him intently.

She quickly explained that she belonged to a very old family in this area and that she lived on the other side of the lagoon, but she was staying in the hotel for a few days. Mampa's voice flowed warm, now with the undulating accent of the locals. Matías, still not sure why she had approached him, but trying to be courteous, commented that he was from Rosario and was passing through, working with a team on a hydrographic project.

"Would you like a coffee, or anything else?" He asked, calling the waiter.

"Just a glass of water, thank you." She settled into the chair. "Please tell me about your job. The natives of this area are very interested to learn about any project that might help conserve the fresh waters' flow to our sea."

Matías had had every intention of finding out more about her, but now he had to oblige by talking about his post-graduate work. Mampa seemed to absorb each word with great interest, her attentive and expressive green eyes focused and interspersing comments that demonstrated a good knowledge of the natural riches of the area. She led the conversation to the flamingos, a species that Matías had studied. Talking about them, Mampa's eyes brightened and her voice intensified.

"This sea has created a special food for our flamingos," she said.

Matías nodded. He knew that in Mar Chiquita, as in the Dead Sea, there is a salt water crustacean that gives the birds that deep pink color that characterizes them as a distinctive variety of both seas.

"So, it is most important that we protect our flamingos," she insisted, her eyes on his. "They are our treasure, the treasure of our sea. Have you visited the area where the Rio Dulce ends?"

He shook his head.

"Please, go and see the estuaries so you can appreciate them in all their splendor. You will see majestic bands of hundreds of flamingos flying in unison. They visit us once a year after flying incredible distances from the Andes Mountains."

Matías nodded absentmindedly, considering when it would be appropriate to ask her about the previous day on the beach, but he dismissed the urge. He did not want to break the spell of a conversation as serious for her as it was unexpected for him. She settled back in her chair.

"Matías," she said softly but urgently. He felt his heart quicken as he heard his name in her melodic voice. "The Rio Dulce is badly managed to the north as it crosses through Santiago del Estero. They divert the waters to other lands, without control. We are experiencing a great drought, and those waters are the life of this sea."

He nodded in silence while she spoke.

"Even if it rains a lot at times," she continued, "the drought is here, and it will get worse. Something must be done so that our sea does not become a sterile salt flat, to which the migratory species will not be able to return. The Pilgrim falcons, arriving every December from Alaska, will not be back. Worse, the flamingos will not return."

She was tense, shaking with a passion that he could not avoid and, inevitably, he had to lock his eyes on hers.

"I do not know what will happen to all of us," she continued, "if our sea slowly turns into a flat salt desert. Migratory birds will have no refuge. Salt storms will shake the area until it gets uninhabitable. The rains will be scarce, and the sea will die slowly."

Matías, moved by her words, tried to explain that he was doing everything possible with this project, but, from his position, he could not influence anyone important directly. She stopped him short, softly but firmly.

"We never know what someone with determination and love for what she or he does is capable of with persistence."

"True, we never know," he agreed, secretly feeling that the only thing that mattered to him was to keep looking at her. He would have liked that moment to stretch forever, both of them like that, linked in a way that was inexplicable and overwhelming.

Her green eyes recovered their initial vivacity and flirtatious spark as if she were reading his thoughts. Their dialogue and her presence all had that unreal quality that he had noticed since waking up from his dream on the beach. He redirected the conversation politely to Miramar, trying without success to find out more about her. Then he invited her to dinner that night, and she accepted, seemingly very pleased.

They parted, and he saw her walking towards the staircase of the hotel. She climbed up with a graceful and elegant step, her dark, undulating hair shining under the room's lights.

Annoyingly, his knees were shaking again. He had noticed that Mampa did not wear rings on her fingers, only a necklace on her discreet neckline made of small, shiny stones, maybe a local craft. She should be single, he thought hopefully.

Matías went up to his room, took a bath and called his companions to tell them that he was going to have dinner with someone else that night. When he went down to the dining room at the time they had agreed, Mampa did not show up. He waited a half hour and finally asked the concierge on duty if he had seen the beautiful guest come down from her room. The man looked at him with surprise.

"No, there is no guest with that name staying here."

Concealing his impatience, he went to the bar, where the same employee of the afternoon shift was still behind the counter.

"No, sir, we haven't seen any lady here that fit that description."

"Impossible," he insisted. "She was here. Please, call the waiter who served me the coffee and brought her water."

The waiter assured him that when he had brought the glass, Matías was alone facing the window and that the chair on the other side of the table was empty.

A tremor again ran from his head to his toes. Something very weird was happening. He thanked the man. Confused and no explanation as to what was happening, he joined the table of his classmates and reluctantly ate a light dinner.

That night he hardly slept, and at times he had nightmares. He woke up with a headache and the day was almost lost reviewing notes while waiting for the wind to subside. Matías could hardly concentrate on his work anyway, obsessed with his strange encounter with Mampa. Finally, at nightfall, the storm passed, and by the next day everything had returned to normal. The beach was bathed in a layer of salt that would eventually mix with the sand of the coast.

Driving in a worn but comfortable Land Rover with a loquacious native guide at the wheel, the trio headed towards the mouth of the Rio Dulce. The beauty of the estuaries left them speechless. They saw flocks of ducks, swans, parrots, herons, and some small mammals.

Matías asked the guide if he knew an old local family by the name of Anzenuza. After thinking a bit, he said no, there was no family he knew of with that name. Before the arrival of the Spaniards four centuries ago, however, the natives of the area, the Sanavirons, had named the lagoon Mar de Anzenuza.

By then the mystery of Mampa had grown, and Matías started to doubt his mental stability.

Their ride that day included a lunch of sandwiches and sodas near the abandoned and supposedly haunted Vienna Hotel. They ate at picnic tables in the shade of immense palm trees, well-maintained for the tourists and evident remnants of an old and vast park surrounding the building. Later, the guide led them through the empty rooms of the abandoned structure. The windows still retained the original folding shutters and had balconies overlooking the sea. The guide explained succinctly:

"This used to be a five-star hotel, built in 1940 and abandoned without any explanation after World War II. People say that strange forms have appeared at night on the balconies, even though the building remains locked after hours."

They walked examining the empty rooms and, indeed, everything there had an enigmatic air of abandonment. Matías stayed behind and leaned out of one of the windows to breathe the cool breeze. He lingered there, looking at the immense lake-sea about two hundred yards away, with its incessant white crests, and the barely visible coast on the other side.

"These are the grounds of the Anzenuza," he thought, with a shudder. Of Mampa Anzenuza, if that was, in fact, a real person and that was her real name.

He was not sure what all this meant; everything surrounding her appearance had seemed so unreal. He leaned out again and felt the dry air caress his feverish forehead. Below, the stones that led to the coast were still mostly covered with salt. A woman walked barefoot on the beach, her hair waving in the wind and her curvy body unmistakable. He recognized Mampa, with her flexible step and the legs that he had so closely admired at the hotel. Without thinking he raised his arm to greet her and she, evidently knowing that he was there, stopped right in front of the building. She looked towards his balcony and returned the greeting waving her hand for a moment, but then continued on her way, not looking back at him.

Matías wanted to scream her name, but he realized she might not hear him at such a distance. He hurried out of the room and flew down the stairs skipping steps. When he reached the exit, he turned at the cross-planted sign that said *Grand Hotel Vienna, A Mystery by The Sea*, and ran towards the stones that led to the beach. There was no one walking there. Only the groups of tourists gathered around their guides were visible under the palm trees. The beach stretched left and right completely deserted, and caressed by the incessant waves.

Matías sat on one of the stones and covered his face with his hands. His heart was pounding, and a feeling of loneliness and exasperation invaded him. His eyes filled with tears and he took a deep breath, surprised at what he was experiencing.

During the rest of the week somehow Matías managed to finish the work with his teammates. Although he hoped to see her, Mampa did not appear again.

Back in Rosario, he researched the lagoon, its history, and the traditions of the area. He learned that in the Sanaviron language, Mampa means waterway, a stream of fresh water, which somehow seemed appropriate for the beautiful and mysterious native woman.

Six months passed, and he totally immersed himself in his job. His team's report, due to its merits, was recommended to a commission working on fresh waters at the United Nations. Meanwhile, the figure of the mysterious woman carved in the wooden statuette sat on his nightstand and was a constant reminder of his strange and inexplicable experience.

One day during a visit to a friend's home, Matías found an old out of print book of traditions and indigenous myths of South America. Flipping through it almost at random, the page opened directly to a legend about the Anzenuza Sea that caught his eye immediately. His heart leaped when he read it:

"Legend says that once upon a time, the sea was an immense fresh water lagoon, inhabited by a beautiful and dazzling Goddess. The only thing that made her favorable to the people of the area was to get the first unconditional love of the men. It is said that a young Indian prince came to its beaches one day after a battle. The Goddess fell in love with him, but the young man was mortally wounded.

"She felt shaken by a cosmic bolt of lightning. In love for the first time, the Goddess understood that he was going to abandon her, and her lament shook the heavens. The sky cried with the Goddess, and the sea convulsed in a furious tempest. At dawn, the young man awoke on the sand, his wounds healed. He looked around and saw that nature had been transformed. The beach was now white and the waters turbid, salty. He remembered having seen a beautiful woman with green eyes and a captivating smile while he thought he was dying.

"He felt healthy and full of energy, and a great force pushed him toward the sea. He waded into the waters and continued swimming until the caress of a pink ray of sunrise transformed him into the elegant flamingo, the eternal guardian of the Sea Goddess."

¡No, of course not!

The nurse at the pharmacy placed the thermometer on the table. "You don't have a fever." Lucia stood up slowly. "What do you have is a very strong cold, so take aspirin and rest. By the way, how is your mom doing?" Lucia smiled doubtfully before answering. "Well... her arm hurts a lot, and the wound has not healed yet."

The nurse sighed and asked with affirmation, almost as if dismissing its importance: "Your mom has cancer, right?" Lucia's skin crawled. She was horrified. "No, please, do not say that. My mother is only recovering from surgery..." The nurse hesitated. Regretting the doubt she had obviously planted in Lucia, who looked at her with alarm, she added almost with guilt: "I'm so sorry, I must have mistaken your mom for another patient." Lucia recovered somewhat. "It's fine," she muttered, forcing a smile, "thank you for taking my temperature today."

Lucia walked out into the street, still stunned by the emotional shock of the forbidden, irrevocable word spoken, and it took a few minutes for her to calm down.

She made her way to the house where her mother was sitting as always in her rocking chair, listening to the afternoon soap opera on the radio, and waiting for the analgesics to work for a few more hours. Then the throbbing, fierce pain would start again, and reprise the endless circle of suffering: Change of blood-soaked bandages, excruciating pain, soothing pills, repeat.

Lucia walked into the living room, kissed her mother tenderly and went straight to the kitchen where her sister, visiting, was helping with dinner. The sweet voice of Nat King Cole crooned in Spanish from the small transistor radio on the counter.

"Tell me, is it true that mom has cancer?" She asked bluntly.

"No! Of course not!" Her sister responded, alarmed.

Lucia sighed with relief.

"I knew that it was not cancer," she said, feeling that everything was regaining its natural order around her.

The monster, again denied, granted another of its wretched truces.

Editor's Note: This micro story, together with the one titled No Answer, were finalists in the literary contest 2015 Microrrelatos Cancer de Mama, organized by Talento Comunicación of Spain, and both appear in the Anthology of the same name.

Bath Bubbles

It has an excellent price, and it is in perfect condition," Fernando said as he parked the car in front of the house.

Celia glanced out the window at the red roof behind which a few trees peeked over. The front yard inclined down to the street and was covered by a lawn freshly washed by the recent rains. It was small but beautiful. They got out of the car.

"Once again, thanks for joining me."

"That's what friends are for," Fernando answered.

"I hope it's the one I'm looking for," Celia crossed her fingers.

"Let's go inside," he said, taking her arm, understanding.

The real estate agent approached them smiling and extended her hand in a professional welcome. They walked in. As Celia stepped into the living room with large windows, something told her yes, this could be the house. His friend made a questioning gesture behind the agent's back, and Celia nodded smiling but added in a whisper: "I don't want to get too excited. Please don't miss any detail of the construction."

They followed the agent in silence, and despite an inner voice that told her not to rush, Celia walked through the rooms with the feeling that she had finally found what she was looking for. The house was small, comfortable, with walls in warm colors. It had everything she could ask for at that price, and it was so inviting.

"The air conditioning system is only two years old, and that's a big advantage," said the woman.

Celia scored that detail as a plus, because with the nerves of signing the divorce papers and her hot flashes, she could not imagine a night without fresh air circulating in her room. The bedroom would never be *theirs* anymore, hers and Carlos'. It had been almost a year since the separation, but the memories were fresh and still hurt. Celia regretted the thought right away. She had to cling to her new life. A new life that had opened up in front of her like an abyss when he confessed that he was leaving her. That he was in love with that brat, young enough to be his daughter. She reminded herself that this was her life from now on. Celia, single, with good friends, but living alone.

"Let's go to the bathroom," the agent said, looking at her with a meaningful smile. "I'm sure you will like the bathroom."

Fernando rolled his eyes mockingly behind her and Celia had to suppress a laugh.

They stopped at the door. The bathroom was spectacular. It was large, with a separate shower, a long, bright vanity and a window that revealed the backyard and a large blooming red hibiscus.

Celia examined the room with wide eyes. The woman knew what she was talking about. Under the window, against the wall, splendid, was the central attraction of the room: a sparkling cream-colored vintage enamel bathtub. It was beautiful. Celina held her breath, and when she looked at Fernando, she noticed he was also impressed.

"This is the icing on the cake, no doubt," he murmured, getting closer, "although it's old."

"But in excellent condition," the agent said quickly, glimpsing sideways at Celia and measuring the impression it had made on her. "Incredibly well kept for how old it must be. It's exquisite, isn't it? Those beautiful legs are a work of art. The old owners must have bought it from an antique shop and paid a good price for it."

In the end, it turned out just like the agent anticipated. Celia counter-offered, they accepted it, and after two months of nonstop activity after work, she managed to move. She downsized her belongings and furniture, and with the help of a couple of friends in a weekend, she was moved in. It was her own first house, her first real estate property.

Busy with work at the office and decorating the new home, time passed without Celia taking the long, restorative bath that had planned before the move. The bottle of soapy bubbles and the lavender-scented candles that she meant use for the immersion bath were still wrapped, just like when she bought them. Carlos's betrayal still hurt, and she blamed herself for not having seen it coming, for trusting that everything was fine between them. Then again, she shouldn't have married him knowing he was a womanizer. It was all her fault.

The nights were cool, comfortable, but sleepless. The memories came back in droves as soon as Celia closed her book and turned off the light. In the mornings she woke up before the alarm rang, and when she looked at herself in the mirror, she saw a worn-down and sad image of herself. A boring and old middle-aged woman.

"You have to do therapy," her friends had told her, those few who could read her thoughts. "You have not been able to overcome what Carlos did to you alone. You need professional help."

At first, they brought her self-help books and magazine articles with good advice to help get her out of the misery she felt, for a long time put in the effort she could muster. She even began, although half-heartedly, a weekly therapy session with a well-recommended therapist.

The bathtub was still there, tempting, but for one reason or another Celia could never get around to investing the time necessary for the long immersion bath she had promised herself. Maybe it was because it brought back memories, something she had discovered while talking to the therapist, although she did not mention it to him. She realized it right in the middle of a session. She was telling him about their honeymoon when she and Carlos had frolicked in the bathtub of a romantic old hotel in Montreal almost ten years ago. She remembered well that that one was a very similar bathtub to the one waiting patiently for her at home.

"How curious, one buries memories, and suddenly they jump at you like a surprise attack," she thought.

Several months after moving, she received an email from Marta, a high school classmate she had reconnected with on Facebook not long ago.

After a series of updates on various topics, Marta added: "By the way. Do you recall Guillermo Linares? Well,

I saw him yesterday by chance. We talked about you. He didn't know that you are divorced. I don't know if you knew, but he also divorced a few years back. Anyway, he mentioned how he had seen you on Facebook. I don't know... he seemed interested in finding out about your life. Maybe he doesn't dare to contact you. He looks good, and he was alone." The message ended with a couple of lines about other matters.

Celia reread the email to be sure she had not misunderstood.

How could she not remember him? Guillermo was her first love, her high school sweetheart, whom she left when they started college and she met Franco. He was a thirty-something Italian hunk who had her charmed for a few months and then he left her when he returned to Milan. She went out to dine and dance with several guys through the years, but none of them meant anything special to her. Certainly none like Guillermo, with his light brown hair and sensual lips. He was the guy all the girls she knew were attracted to, but she had left for an exotic and passing whim. Later she met Carlos, fell in love and they married.

She opened her Facebook account and hesitated for a moment hovering over the search bar in the upper left corner, before carefully typing Guillermo Linares. Then, as if by magic, his picture appeared on the screen. Celia concentrated on it for a few minutes, tracing those familiar features that now, over the years, had changed slightly, benefiting him with an air of maturity that she thought, with unexpected delight, suites him very well. She reviewed the page and found photos and comments from unknown people, but she didn't care about further details. "Maybe he doesn't dare to contact you," Marta had written. Without thinking further, she sent him a friend request and leaned on the back of the chair with a sigh. OK. It could not be undone even if she wanted to. Celia returned to Marta's message and reread it, paying careful attention to each word.

When she closed it, she needed a glass of wine. There was a half a bottle of Torrontés in the fridge, and Celia chose a large glass. While making a salad for dinner, the image of Guillermo returned to her vividly. Had she forgotten him? Almost. She realized she had not thought about those years before marriage for a long, long time.

It was Friday, early in the evening and she was not tired. She put a movie on during dinner, but did not pay attention, lost in her thoughts. What a coincidence, she remembered, the last time she had seen Guillermo was in the most unusual place, in the restaurant of that hotel in Montreal. He was having dinner with a group of colleagues from a technology conference. They exchanged a couple of words, and she introduced him to Carlos, her newly wedded husband. When they had parted, she had felt sorry for him, for the sad way he looked at her. She was hanging on Carlos' arm, totally drunk with happiness and plans for the future. Guillermo was single and was with colleagues and their partners. So, he also got married later and ended up in divorce...

Celia turned off the TV, put on a CD of Chopin and walked to the bathroom. Without closing the door, she searched for the candles and bubbles and prepared herself meticulously for the bath she had postponed for so long.

While the warm water filled the enameled and gleaming basin, Celia lingered before her antique mirror, which matched the bathroom style and created a subtle and elegant air of the eighteen hundreds. "Like the one in that Montreal hotel," she told herself.

She dropped her robe and flirtatiously released the professional hairdo. Her brown, straight hair went down her shoulders framing her face. She looked at herself naked for a long time, satisfied with her slender body in spite of its almost five decades while forming a loose bun with her hair and fixing it high on her head with a clasp.

"This hairstyle matches the decoration of the bathroom better," Celia noted with a smile. She poured the pink liquid soap into the stream of water, and the bubbles began to form, light, immense, and colorful until they covered the surface of the water. Then she switched off the light; the twinkling of the candles emitted an amber glow. Finally, she turned off the tap and climbed in, sliding to rest her head on the edge of the tub. She reached for her glass and took a whiff of her wine.

Celia felt relaxed, and a pleasurable calm invaded her. She sipped some of the wine, listened to the music that came from her living room and set out to enjoy the sensual piano and the long-awaited immersion bubble bath. She thought of Guillermo, of the memories she had of him. She remembered his young naked body, on the bed of his room, where they used to enter tiptoeing, furtive, through the back door of his parent's house. And of that night when, with the moonlight shining on the skin of intertwined legs after making love, he had assured her:

"from today on, every time you see a moonbeam enter this way through a window, you will remember me."

Up high, behind the dark hibiscus, the moon shone silvery and distant. A moonbeam that seeped through the branches reflected multiple little dots of color on the soap bubbles that covered her knees protruding from the water.

Then Celia closed her eyes and realized why that bathtub had chosen her.

Agnese

The embroidery needle sticks on the firm surface of linen again. Agnese tugs distractedly on the bright red thread that after many ups and downs will fill the petals of a rose that her sister Angela has drawn in pencil on the fabric. She wants to peek at the window, but she has already done so several times that afternoon, and Agnese has no more excuses to spy yet again on the empty cobblestones scorching under the implacable January sun.

And yet, he is there, across the street, looking out of his workshop's window. Those intense dark eyes that devoured Agnese during the ten-o'clock mass on so many Sundays anxiously looking for another furtive gaze or guilty smile. Their racing hearts had throbbed under dampened shirts, her chest heaving under the stiff corset and high lace neckline, both almost suffocating in the church's hot and incense-smoked air.

"Maurizio... Maurizio," she whispers his name tenderly.

Agnese wonders how his voice sounds. What inflections would that voice have when calling her name with a Genoa accent? Will they ever get to talk face to face? She imagines herself in front of Maurizio, trembling and with nothing to say. Thinking of him takes her breath away, and she feels new things, like those delicious and unexpected shudders that her instinct tells her are forbidden. That's why she never talks about it, not even with her sisters. What would Angela say if she knew? Agnese frowns and rejects the thought. Angela is distant. Berta would have understood, but now she is too busy with her married life, and since the wedding, without explanation, she had stopped confiding in Agnese. Berta's eyes now hint at something that nobody else seems to have noticed; a wise spark, a glow that reminds Agnese of her sister's expression on birthdays or at Christmas when Berta opened her gifts. Something must happen on a wedding night. Agnese is sure of it now; if only she could find out what it is.

Berta is happy, and she has earned it. Agnese wishes she had been born with that same strength of character to challenge her father. When her parents opposed their courtship, her sister declared herself ill and stayed in bed without eating for more than a week. She only sipped water until the family doctor said that if she was not allowed to marry, the girl could die of sadness and starvation. And Tata conceded, as was always the case when her sister threw a tantrum about something. Mamma protested and repeated, again, and again that the suitor's reputation was questionable at best, but she could not win against the combined pressure exerted by her daughter and her fiancé's family. Now Berta shines, lives in her own house and Agnese has not only lost her one confidant but gained a brother-in-law that winks at her behind her sister's back and approaches her provocatively when they are alone, making her feel acutely uncomfortable.

The embroidered rose is taking shape, covered by identical, disinterested stitches, while Agnese counts the minutes before returning to the window without raising suspicion. Mamma fans herself slowly as she reads a page of the *Vocce d'Italia* newspaper that Tata left in the room. Angela writes in her private diary, and little Armando sleeps peacefully on the sofa, hugging Caruso, who purrs indolently. The lemonade in the pitcher on the table lost the coolness the water had when it was taken out of the large ceramic jug that rests in the shade at the back gallery. It is a siesta like so many others, endless, with that unbearable humid heat that rises from the Paraná River and covers the city of Rosario like a dense and suffocating mantle. The light curtain on the window barely moves, gently rustled by the scarce air that runs through the wide-open windows and doors of the house.

The cuckoo clock marks the minutes, and Agnese misses the pencil line repeatedly as she stitches waiting for another fifteen minutes to approach the window, when the beautiful and unexpected sound of the barrel street organ approaching makes her jump out of her chair. Caruso flinches and leaps off the couch, attentive.

"Mamma, the organ grinder! Should I beckon him to stop at our door?" Asks Agnese, already squeezing the light curtain with a trembling hand and looking towards the window across the street, flushing, her heart beating with joy because he is there, waiting for her. He tips his head toward her, and from afar she feels his eyes burning through her.

"Sure, and please ask him to play a waltz for us," her mother replies smiling.

"Pañuelito Blanco," says Angela without raising her head, hurrying to finish her paragraph to lean out of the window too. "Ask for *Pañuelito Blanco*, please." But Agnese does not hear her, concentrating on the black eyes that

induce in her vertigo, bliss, laughter, and tears, all at once.

At night Tata exchanges mysterious glances and comments with Mamma during dinner, but since children do not speak at the table unless they are addressed, nobody breaks the silence. Agnese has the impression that her sister knows what this is all about, as Doménico and Carlos, her older brothers, make faces at Angela. She shushes them with a discreet headshake.

Mamma signals Caterina, who ceremoniously removes the dessert plates. It is the time of the evening when Tata lights his cigar, so the boys get up from the table. Agnese gets ready to follow them.

"We have to talk to you, Añé," Tata says in that tone that always makes her shiver. Mamma makes kindly winks at her, reassuring her. Angela and the others leave giggling mysteriously.

Carmelo sits down on his chair. Unhurriedly, he opens the box of cigars and begins his nightly ritual, taking a little longer than usual in cutting the cigar, searching for words until finally he lights it, clears his throat and looks at his daughter face to face.

"*Donna* Giovanna is coming to visit us tomorrow. She approached me today at the store."

Agnese's skin bristles. Why is he talking about *Donna* Giovanna? She is the matchmaker, the woman who intercedes when a good Italian boy is in love and wants to get married. Perhaps Maurizio? No, it's not possible, she must be dreaming. Tata would never want to hear anything about him. She knows that the stolen glances at Mass and from the window are sinful because Maurizio will never dare to speak to her in the open. Not because he is a tailor, an honorable profession in the eyes of her father. Because he is the son of a single woman, a sinner who has dared to give birth to what they call a bastard, who has challenged the whole world by living alone and raising Maurizio with her head held high and no apologies. The worst type of woman, the daughter of a good family that took a wrong step in life.

Agnese has been listening to that story since she was a child and does not fool herself for a moment. Old Giovanna comes to meddle for another suitor, inevitably. Agnese feels a lump in her throat. She is afraid of the tears that are coming and breathes deeply, although late. Her mother palms her hand tenderly and smiles, but that does not reassure her at all. Mamma and Tata act in unison and almost always share the same opinion.

"Donna Giovanna is trustworthy, dear; I'm sure she has a good candidate for you," she says.

"Mamma, I don't want to, I don't want to get married!" At last the watery blue eyes melt into tears.

"You are already sixteen, Agnese, Why do you complain?" Tata goes back to his chair, annoyed. The Calabrian dialect in which he speaks at home acquires that fast and strongly accented rhythm that predicts a storm. "You are no longer a little girl; you are a woman now."

"Angela gets married in three months," Mamma intervenes, "and then it will be your turn. It seems he's a good boy. His name is Aversa, Carmelo Aversa. He recently arrived from Italy and already has a small carriage and a horse, and he opened a butcher shop in a big market in Córdoba."

Anguish chokes her. Córdoba? So far away from Rosario? In Córdoba, there are still Indians. It's a nightmare; this cannot be happening to her. At last, she gathers enough energy to speak, trembling:

"Tata, Mamma, please, don't do this. Tata, you threw the gypsies out when they came to the store so many times wanting to buy me when that gypsy kid became infatuated with me. Do you remember? Tell Donna Giovanna that you do not want me to marry yet. That I am too young. Tata, please!"

He smiles, remembering with sympathy the stubborn chief of the gypsy tribe who, a couple of years ago, had insisted on buying Agnese for his son, in love with her hopelessly. The kid had good taste he thought, choosing the most beautiful of his daughters. Good people and cunning, those gypsies, if you knew how to negotiate with them, but not good enough to belong in the family, of course. Nomads are unhygienic in their habits, moving from one place to another, like the Indians of the pampas, and they spoke with an unpleasant, guttural language. They were very similar to those gypsies he knew in Calabria.

He turns his attention to Agnese, who still looks at him imploringly.

"Not another word. The matter is done and finished." His dialect words come out even faster and clearly exasperated. "This young man is a good candidate, and I see no reason to snub him. And you should behave better; you look like a child crying like that. You should feel happy. Start preparing the bridal dowry. I don't want to hear any more complaints."

Imperiously, he indicates that they retire. Mamma gets up from her chair at once, making signaling to her daughter, who still looks at her father in despair although she does not dare to challenge his order. Both leave the dining room, closing the door carefully behind them.

Donna Giovanna arrives to visit two days later with the candidate. They go to the dining room. Lemonade and homemade cookies are served. Agnese, with her heart oppressed with anguish and fear, spies the stranger through the keyhole of the dining room door, trying to listen to the conversation. She hears hearty laughs inside. Catarina comes out of the room, after leaving a little tray with few glasses of liquor, and whispers to her that the young man is not so bad, although he is older than her by at least ten years. He doesn't say much and does not seem to know much Spanish. Not that it matters, because in the house only the Calabrian dialect is spoken, and the family speaks Italian when they are in the company of compatriots from other Italian provinces.

"He's honest and ambitious," her father says afterwards, "and he comes from Cosenza. His name is Aversa, from a good family. The Aversas have land there and raise goats and sheep."

And the conversation is over.

Once the date of the wedding is decided, the shy suitor starts visiting her. The two youngest children are always at hand, in case Mamma has to leave the room. Agnese barely looks at her fiancée as she embroiders a piece of her bridal trousseau. Her heart and thoughts are fixated on Maurizio and on the impossible love that she is now forced to drown forever. "It's for your own good,"

Angela and Berta say over and over. Of course, for them it is easy, being in love and happy as they are. Still, they do not tell her anything about the wedding night, nor does she dare to ask.

Despite her hidden terror, on Monday, October 14, 1907, the date of the civil marriage ceremony arrives inescapably. The following Saturday, the 19th, the Christian wedding, and the betrothal party will take place. The bride has her bridal trousseau ready thanks to the close supervision of Mamma and the contribution of her sisters, who flutter enthusiastically around. The impending wedding gives them an opportunity to fill the house with lights, music, and friends.

The civil ceremony takes place on a sunny spring morning. Tata has left his employees in charge of the warehouse and, as he did for the weddings of his eldest daughters, he has organized a copious lunch in the large patio of the house.

As in a dream, Agnese responds affirmatively to the question of the Justice of the Peace. Then, with a trembling hand, she writes her name in the large book. When the father's turn comes, he authorizes Berta's husband to sign on his behalf, because despite how successful he has been and still is in his businesses, he has never wanted to learn to read and write.

The days that follow the ceremony pass by too fast for her. There is ample hubbub in the preparations for the party. Siblings and family members collaborate so that everything is ready on Saturday, following the routine of previous marriages. She feels like a strange, involuntary protagonist of an event that makes everyone else happy, but that fills her with fear and anguish. In the evenings she asks for valerian tea, which helps her to sleep.

On the day of the wedding, Agnese leaves the house where she was born dressed in her bright black brocade wedding gown, in the style of Calabria. Her light brown hair is gathered in two loose waves around her face, tied back in a high bun. Her pale cheeks are hidden under a bit of blush that Berta has applied, expertly, with a piece of cotton and soft pats under the cheekbones. The neighbors gather on the sidewalk, in front of the door, as is customary to greet and admire the bride. She prepares to look one last time at Maurizio, sure that she will see him there.

Grabbing Tata's arm, Agnese inches forward toward the open carriage that awaits them. She sits, and after adjusting her dress, hoop skirt, and petticoat, her eyes dart across the street to his house. There he is, watching her as she expected. Maurizio has the balcony doors wide open, and he is looking at her, defiant, his arms wide and hands resting on the frames. The oppression Agnese feels in her chest now is almost unbearable. Since Carmelo's first visit to her house, she had ceased the secret, silent exchanges of glances and smiles between them. His fierce black eyes, now questioning and hurt, and her moist and submissive pale-blue eyes make contact for the last time across the street.

A couple of seconds before turning her gaze to the neighbors who greet her with blessings and affectionate "Long live the bride!" Agnese notices that Maurizio's angular cheeks gleam with the tears that from now on she will no longer be able to cry for him.

Editor's Note: *Agnese* is a fragment of *The Italians*, one of the three parts in which the book *Del Mediterráneo al Plata* is divided. It narrates the history of the immigration of the author's Italian and Spanish ancestors to Argentina.

Moonlit Night In the Pacific

After nodding off on another of the many catnaps of this trip in the narrow and uncomfortable seats, Luciana and I got up to go to the bathroom. The tiny rooms at the end of the aisle were occupied, and we stood in line in front of them with a resigned sigh, trying not to hinder the flight attendants' path.

"What are those white spots down there, Pablo?" she asked, leaning over the airplane window, her gaze suspended between the few clouds visible below.

"Those are the Pacific waves," I said, distracted. "I can't wait to get there. I wonder how long for Papeete?"

"Well... it will be a while, I reckon. Ask the flight attendant," she said looking at the waves and the misty, gray line where the sky and the Pacific merged. "What a strange day!" Luciana added. "Although I enjoy having such a long sunset, it is surreal. On second thought, since we left Lima things have not been normal, don't you think? This plane in the middle of nowhere... the buzz of the engine... this afternoon that never ends and the sun hanging for hours just above the horizon without deciding to go down. Strange." And after a few seconds: "What if French Polynesia never appears in the ocean? It is almost as if we have crossed to another side, to another dimension..."

"Don't be foolish! What do you mean we have crossed to another dimension?" I replied, annoyed because when she starts rambling out loud, the fantasies grow and grow and if I don't cut those musings short, I end up tangled in her tales. More than once she strung me along with her imagination, but now I take charge before she sucks me in. The last thing I needed right now is to believe that Polynesia got lost in space.

"You are so unimaginative," she complained, annoyed. "It was just a thought."

We were silent for a few seconds, and she started again:

"Did you notice how Sandra changed since we boarded the plane? She looks strange, like upset... she doesn't even talk to us."

"She's nervous because she is leaving everything to get married on the other side of the planet with a man she barely knows... but Kruno is a good guy. It's going to be all right." I said, always conciliatory, although I had no idea how the actual Kruno would be, after his stint as a volunteer in Vietnam.

"I don't know, this girl is acting strangely. She's afraid, or something has changed her," she insisted.

"There, one is available, you go in first," I said, relieved because the little door to the tiny bathroom opened. Also because it interrupted that absurd conversation, a consequence of the exhaustion and the long hours sitting tight in that uncomfortable Air France plane, which for short flights may have been fine, but to cross the ocean expanse between the beaches of Peru and Tahiti was claustrophobic.

Hours later, our heavy backpacks on, we were standing in a line in front of the Papeete Airport counter. As soon as we deplaned to breathe in the humid, hot air of the island, the sun set below the horizon, at last. The Tahitians drew our attention with their strange attire: formal white shirt with a tie, straight skirt printed with large colorful flowers below the knees, black shoes, and three-quarter white socks. On the other hand, we, Argentines and Uruguayans of the immigrant group chartered by the Australian Embassy that November of 1974, wore classic blue jeans and discreet shirts in neutral tones.

We were a tired delegation of haggard and pale nomads, desperate to lie horizontally on a bed. The weight of the bags, backpacks, and packages that we dragged with us, to avoid the surcharge of the extra luggage dispatched on departure, added its share of suffering to what we already carried on our souls for having left everything we knew and had behind.

"Who speaks English here?"

The authoritative voice of a Tahitian man with shiny dark skin and Asian eyes startled us all. A friendly young woman named Jenny, belonging to the group of Uruguayans and traveling with her husband, came forward. Luciana followed her almost without thinking, of course. The two negotiated in English with the agent. The others looked on, expectantly. After a few minutes, the girls came back.

"In a while, they will take us all to the hotel where we are going to spend the night," Luciana said to the whole group, already in the role of commanding general. She changes the tone and volume of her voice when in command function. "Tomorrow after breakfast we'll leave in an Air New Zealand jumbo-jet for Auckland, New Zealand, and from there we'll get on a Quantas airplane for Sydney. The Australians have everything well organized," they both agreed, smiling.

Our eyes widened in awe. None of us had flown in a jumbo-jet yet. It was one of those large, brand-new and double-decked novel aircraft. Moreover, I guessed that some of our fellow travelers might not even have flown at all before this trip.

We were transferred to the hotel in a comfortable bus with the luxury of air conditioning. The moon shone above, and we could see the palm trees under those incredible stars hanging from the black, South Pacific sky.

Our lodging turned out to be a tourist brochure come true, illuminated by oil lamps, yellow-orange flares that rippled in the breeze. Each cabin had a stone path, and we could see the beach beyond them, illumined by the moonlight. We had to tread the pathways carefully, so as not to crush the thousands of snails that wandered around everywhere.

They took us to our cabin, a hut like the others; thatched roof and bamboo or wooden walls. My tiredness disappeared instantly. I looked forward to taking advantage of that short visit to paradise, and we would rest after the romance.

"How come! Are the three of us not sharing the same cabin?" The irritated voice of our bad-tempered travel companion made me jump. Sandra had not opened her mouth since we left Lima.

I looked at her intrigued. What did she mean by that? The Tahitian guide had placed her in the cabin of an elderly Uruguayan woman who was traveling with a young couple. Like a capricious girl, her eyes filled with tears. Luciana and I looked at each other in alarm, but the Tahitian guide politely insisted and steered her toward the rest of the group. We sighed with relief.

"See you for dinner," I said, elusive. Luciana patted Sandra's shoulder, sympathizing with her, but said nothing. Luciana seemed hurt by her friend's inexplicable and hostile silence of so many hours. And, frankly, by then I was also tired of her.

There was time for a quick hot shower before we all gathered in the dining room. In half an hour the group of grumpy travelers had been renewed, and with lighter clothes and a drink, we were all in an excellent mood. Except for Sandra, of course, who glared at us with her sharp reproachful look across the table. Luciana and I tried to ignore her. After all, we were in paradise, and we wanted to take a walk on the beach with the others before diving into the crisp white sheets of our cozy tropical bedroom.

I was thinking about what drinks I was going to ask room service to bring to the hut. It was going to be a special night, one of those I had imagined so many times looking at tourist brochures of the Pacific islands, back at my little apartment in Buenos Aires.

Half an hour later I was lying on the bed, reclining on the high pillows, smoking and about to call for drinks.

Hawaiian guitars sounded sweetly from the speaker on the wall next to the night table. Just like in my dreams.

Luciana had finished giving me a tempting modeling show with the new bikini that she was going to wear at the beach as soon as we arrived in Melbourne when I heard the rapid, annoying knocks on the door. I jumped out of bed while Luciana covered herself with one of my shirts. When I opened it I found Sandra's face, bathed in tears. I stepped aside to let her come in, mentally cursing my bad luck.

After crying for what seemed an eternity threatening suicide while we soothed her, Sandra fell asleep on the sofa in front of our bed. Luciana and I looked at each other full of frustration. Soon it was going to be time to leave for the airport. The sheets were still crisp and immaculate, and the room service of drinks was not yet made.

We stood silently and began to put our clothes back in our bags, smothering dark criminal impulses while glancing at the angelic face of our friend, who slept peacefully, curled up on the sofa.

"See?" Luciana said, triumphant. "I told you so! Something weird is happening on this trip. Something is not normal. To think that you never, ever believe my hunches!"

Then we looked at each other over the open bags on the bed. We were again haggard, weary with fatigue and looking pathetic. We must have both thought the same thing about each other at that moment because we laughed in unison.

Sandra muttered something, turned around and continued to sleep soundly.

Sex Appeal

Ignacio told me to keep my eyes closed. I reached out blindly and clung to the heavy curtain he had pulled with a mischievous smile. The place smelled of a mixture of incense and fresh paint.

"And do not move," he added in his Gregorian chant voice, leaving me alone in the dark at the entrance to the room. Surely this is another of his stunts to impress me, I thought, like his father's Ferrari, or that cocktail party full of TV personalities at the yacht club, where he took me last Saturday.

I was not fooled by his attempts to make me forget his round baby face with gifts, tickets to shows and access to exclusive places. For him, I was a Cinderella, pretty, curvy and striking but very poor, who looked at his world from the other side of the window, my nose stuck against the glass. He would show me off everywhere, basking in the role of the prince... although a prince still in the pond, minus the kiss and the transformation, let's say.

I opened my eyes and let go of the curtain. Some echoes were audible from the semi-dark of the empty disco, and suddenly, with an explosion of deafening sound and light, the vault of the hall revealed itself. I took a step back, startled. It was more than a regular nightclub. It was huge and very modern, with all the electronic equipment on, just for me. Ignacio approached me, laughing like a naughty child. He was holding his hand outstretched, looking at me, inviting. He knew how to attract me, I thought, and make me forget his uneven teeth and his plump figure.

With a confident stride, he guided me to the dance floor, moving with unexpected grace to the tune of rock n' roll. Next up was a romantic bolero to dance cheek to cheek, except with us, his cheek was closer to my shoulder.

"My old man is going to Europe tomorrow," he murmured, "and I'm going to have the Ferrari for several days."

I shuddered with delight, and he noticed. The envy the girls are going to feel, I thought. Those narrow-minded and jealous friends of mine.

"We can go wherever you want," he added. I pressed against him, eyes closed, imagining the scent of rich leather on the soft seats of the car, satellite navigation, digital music, and the forced smiles of my envious friends. He squeezed my waist a little more as if he knew.

"Can I invite my friends to the opening of the nightclub?" I asked, gloating. "Of course you can. And if you finally come to my apartment tonight, you can choose another gift," he added. Then standing on his tiptoes, gave me a chaste and mentholated kiss, without demands, on the lips.

"I like that red Dior, the one with the plunging neckline we saw today in the Fendi window," I said, and with a determined move I leaned over his captive prince's face like a malevolent spell and whispered, "So, let's go pick it up."

His eyes sparkled with the implicit promise and the expectation of that night.

Aunt Lusa

My sister's voice broke again in a sob, and I, who always spoke for both of us, kept silent this time. It was a guilty silence, for not being able to be there at her side, sharing the pain of saying goodbye to yet another member of the family. "Just as it happened with mom and dad," I thought, "so many years ago. Now history repeats itself. "

"Lusa does not recognize me anymore," Rosita said with worry. "She thinks I'm Grandma. She talks to her mother with more anger than ever, about things that I do not even know. Sometimes she sounds like a young girl screaming reproaches to her..."

"I'm so sorry, but calm down, please, and take it easy. You can't do more than you already do, remember that she has Alzheimer's. Poor soul, the connections in her brain are malfunctioning."

My sister cried for a while, and I waited on this side of the line, many miles away to the north, for her to calm down again. When she vented her sorrow and I felt that she was calm, we said goodbye and hung up.

I wiped my tears of frustration and guilt and went to prepare something for dinner. While cooking, my thoughts took me several decades back in time, again at my parents' house.

After Grandma Inés died, my aunt Lucía, Lusa to the family, was left alone and Mom invited her to live with us. Dad did not object, although I knew that he never liked the idea very much because one day I heard him say: "She a bit bitter."

Mom brought her home, as Lusa was her younger sister, but also because she had always been different from her other sisters, sort of helpless, a little distracted and even somewhat obsessive. Still unmarried at thirty-something, pretty, with a mane of dark wavy hair and beautiful green eyes, her mother had told her more than once, as if it were a natural and established fact: "You are not going to marry, Lusa. Guys will laugh at your leg," alluding to the slight limp that polio left her when she was three years old.

When Lusa used to recall things like that, my sister and I would look at each other in silence and think how callous, how hurtful it was. It seemed incredible to us that our Grandma, whom I adored, could have said such a thing.

When Grandma fell ill with breast cancer, Lusa devoted all her free time to taking care of her for three long years. She started in the mornings, very early, then she left for work and run back in the afternoon to tend to her. I do not know how Lusa took those cruel words at the time, or what she would have answered to her mother, or if she ever answered, but I know they marked her forever. Lusa did not have any social life after her working hours, not even when she moved in with us. Once, she dated a man for a few months who in the end turned out to be married. Upon finding out, she broke the relationship. We learned about the details of this story much later, through discreet comments made by our mother.

Lusa would work at home, leaning over the Singer sewing machine that had been part of Grandma's wedding trousseau at the beginning of the century. I remember Lusa cutting and sewing pants for Severo Humeres, a meticulous tailor from downtown. Severo was a gentle Bolivian man who valued neat stitching and to whom I, for several years in my early teens, delivered Lusa's quality finished work once a week. I was allowed to travel on the bus by myself, something that made me feel very grownup and important.

Throughout the years that she lived in our house, Aunt Lusa also sewed for Rosita and I dresses, coats, skirts, most of our clothes actually, while ruminating on her memories in the kitchen during so many afternoons sipping mate with mom and my sister.

My mother was an innate feminist, born long before the word feminism appeared on our horizon. She was always open to new ideas, intellectually curious and many times we heard her say: "When you hear that the old times were better, do not believe it. The future is going to be better. It's going to have so many things that I'm not going to see and that you two will enjoy..." And I knew that the past for her meant the thirties, the years of the big Depression and deprivation. The future for her was the marvelous advances she could sense reading books and articles from the United States in *The Reader's Digest* in Spanish. And I could feel in my veins that expectation, those possibilities that my mother dreamed for us.

At our afternoon kitchen gatherings, my sister, Mom and I discussed movies, books, and magazine articles as if we were deciding the fate of the world. We did it in a serious-minded manner, with eagerness and passion. But Lusa did not participate with likewise enthusiasm. She always had something that stopped her from dreaming big. She saw something negative, something dangerous in everything that was new and unknown. She could not fly with her imagination and distrusted our friends, men in general, and the world.

One day we understood her reasons, when we found Lusa surrounded by albums and boxes of family photos. Silently and methodically, she was tearing one by one the valuable and unique sepia and black and white photographs that the family had collected for almost a century.

Lusa did not stop until she destroyed each one of them, oblivious of our despair. Not even the impressive wedding portrait of our grandparents, Inés and Carmelo, was saved. In the chaos, we managed to sneak two or three photos in secret, but the annihilation of her past was physical, symbolic and complete.

From that day on she never again revisited the graves of her parents. Many years later, when the cemetery where they were buried, sent a letter to her stating that their remains were going to be disposed of in a common grave for lack of payment, she tore the letter, threw it in the trash can and kept talking about something else.

Lusa destroyed the pictures, but she could not detach herself from the painful bindings tightly knotted in her mind. She suffered from claustrophobia and just to think that one day she would be put to rest in a closed coffin, or worse, be buried underground, made her shudder with panic. Mom reassured her, like a daughter.

When my sister and I started going out to parties with friends, Lusa decided to move to a boarding house for women in downtown Córdoba. But she would come home daily; she was always close to us. Lusa was both a slightly eccentric older sister and an old maid who had strictly forbidden us to talk about her age with anyone.

The years passed, and she shared our joys and sorrows, our weddings, and to my sister's children she was a dear and reliable substitute grandmother. Lusa was also at the family side when I, always living in a foreign country or another, was not there for my parents' funerals. Those memories brought tears to my eyes.

Rosita told me that she no longer recognized her and in each call, I could hear the anguish in her voice. I felt guilty. I am the older sister, and it was as if I had burdened her with all the painful things that distance had shielded me from, such as being present for the last minutes of those we love.

A week later, my sister was on the phone again with her sad news: "I don't know what to do. Lusa does not eat and cries all day. Now she doesn't even get out of bed. I don't know if she is lucid, or if she hears us, but I believe she, somehow, knows that her mind has gone away." And again I found no words to respond. Rosita added: "She is curled up in a fetal position, and the nurses find it difficult to wash her and change her clothes."

The images were horrible, but the worst was to hear the pain in my sister's voice. I calmed her down as I could, but at such a distance, everything I said sounded insufficient. So I admitted to her my feelings of guilt, and she was the one who comforted me and thanked me for being on the other side of the tube whenever she needed me.

Our calls became more frequent. There were changes in medication and new treatments, but we both knew that there was no hope.

A couple of months later, on a Sunday, she called me with urgency: "They are taking her on an ambulance to the hospital. She collapsed, it seems that it's her heart."

A few hours later, Rosita called again to tell me that our aunt had suffered cardiac arrest. She had died suddenly. The doctor told the family that it was the best thing that could have happened. That many Alzheimer's sufferers remain in bed for decades. Lusa had not wanted to cling to life, I thought, a life that after all she never enjoyed very much.

Rosita was inconsolable. "What hurts me more than anything is not to have been able to help her, to rescue her from so much fear, not to have been able to eliminate her terrors and the imaginary visitors who hounded her to the end," she told me, sobbing.

Later Rosita decided to cremate her remains. Her children looked at her with doubt, so my sister called me to get a feel for my thoughts. Lusa had not left anything written about it. "What do you think?" she asked.

"I agree with your decision," I said firmly." Lusa didn't want to be buried anywhere."

"I'm glad you are with me," she said with relief. "I wouldn't want to bury her in a tomb, but I wasn't sure what to do."

"Yes, you are," I said. "Allow her to fly free. Now she is finally not tied to anything any longer. Scatter her ashes in some beautiful place, a field, a lake, anywhere wide, where Lusa can run free."

We cried together for a while, remembering her. It was the first of many moments we shared like that. We owed that to our aunt. It was the best tribute we could give her. I wished with all my heart I could be with my sister for the farewell.

By the time she hung up, my sister had a resolute and self-assured tone in her voice.

Accompanied by her husband and her youngest son, Rosita took the ashes to the high hills of Córdoba, far from it all. They chose a beautiful place from the many that are there and, after saying a farewell prayer, they scattered the ashes on a rushing, cold river.

When my sister, in tears, told me the details, I imagined Lusa as a wave of thin light, floating over the water, gentle as the breeze, liberated from her mental bonds, from her leg with polio, from all her bad memories.

Free from all the things that ought to have been but never were.

A Lengthy Farewell

The train left the Ljubljana station lazily, and Angela struggled to hold back her tears. She swallowed with difficulty and tried to take a deep breath. The memories of the last few days assaulted her without mercy or order, a flow of overwhelming emotions for a girl that had just turned twelve. She hesitantly looked at Aunt Pepsa sitting next to her with her face in her hands, still crying for her brother who had refused to accompany them to Italy.

Uncle Frantz had decided at the last minute to stay to fight the Germans invaders. Impulsively, he lifted his small suitcase and jumped off the carriage that was transporting them from their grandparents' home, the Banić farm to the city. Aunt Pepsa had implored, and Angela cried emphatically, but Frantz marched back resolutely. The girls, taken by surprise and not knowing what to do, had asked the driver to wait, just in case. He turned around once, waving a last good-bye with his hand held high.

Frantz had walked about three hundred yards toward the farm when they saw a squad of German soldiers coming out of the roadside bushes to detain him. The driver, alarmed, had spurred the horses while they, kneeling on the seat and looking back, watched with horror how Uncle Franz disappeared in a bend of the road, pushed by the armed German soldiers that took him who knows where.

Angela felt the twinge of pain again and looking out of the train window, she tried to think of something else while the city was left behind and the familiar landscape of the Slovenian cornfields somehow calmed her internal tumult.

Everything had begun that fateful morning, only a few days ago, when a snake scared Angela on her way to the fields where Anton, her father, worked with the other men. She had given them a basket with freshly baked cheese strudel and quickly raced back to the house, still trembling, to the shelter of Alojzija's maternal arms.

That same night she had heard her parents talk about the surgery scheduled for Aunt Pepsa in Italy. It was meant to improve her leg from the consequences of polio that had forced her to walk with a cane since childhood.

Angela now remembered how her heart had gripped with fear at hearing that she, being the oldest child, and Uncle Frantz the youngest brother, would accompany Aunt Pepsa to Italy. To another world! Far from the farm and everything she knew and loved. Far away from her sisters Justi and Vida, and from Slavka, the little one. She had cried in silence all night, and in the morning, when her parents told her about it during breakfast, she knew that the decision was final. Nobody challenged Anton Martincić, a tall former Prussian soldier, authoritarian, with a quick temper and an iron fist he didn't hesitate to use on anyone. Even Alojzija lowered her head before his commands.

Angela had run to the Banić's farm across the fields, crying inconsolably. Grandma Marija had calmed her down with her usual tenderness. Sitting Angela on her lap until the tears subsided, she had explained why she should accompany Aunt Pepsa and Uncle Frantz and promised that it would not be for long. A few months, if that, she said.

They had spent the morning reading, writing and singing, as always. That was the last time Angela ever saw her grandmother, and she was so happy that she almost forgot her encounter with the snake and the terrifying news of the trip.

Modena, May 1945
Dragi Mama,

How are you all doing at home? Aunt Pepsa and I are fine. How is Dad's leg? Has the wound healed? Tell him to take care of himself and not go to the forest alone, because the Germans will confuse him with a partisan again. Who would have thought that we couldn't go back after Aunt Pepsa's surgery? We have already spent three years here, and now we will have to move again. The Italian government ordered all foreigners to register at Campo Libero, and they are going to drive us to Bologna. We don't know what to do. We can choose to go to Argentina, but we are not sure. I want to go back home, Mama!

In Modena things are very bad, the bombings demolished part of the city to the ground. They killed Il Duce last month, and it seems that everything will change again. Aunt Pepsa wants to go back home too, and I want

*to celebrate my fifteenth birthday there next month, Mama.
I pray every day to be able to see you all soon. I miss
Grandma, our house and our nights embroidering around
the fire.*

Hello to all from Aunt Pepsa.

We love you all very much.

Ángela

Campo Bagnoli, Napoli, July 1949

Dragi Mama,

*I don't write to you as much as I used to, but I'm always
thinking of you and my sisters. They are so grown-up and
beautiful! We received the photos. We are doing well here, in
Campo Bagnoli. We have a little apartment for both of us, and
Aunt Pepsa might have told you in her letters that Rodolfo is
the supervisor of our building. He is a nice man, and Aunt
Pepsa suggested I should marry him. So I did. We had dinner
with friends and then we went on a short honeymoon to Capri,
near Napoli. Mama, Aunt Pepsa and I were very sorry when
you asked us not to return home when the war ended. I cried a
lot, but I know you and the family are not happy with Tito and
the communists there. Pray and have faith.*

*We are working on our papers to go to Buenos Aires as
you told us. The Red Cross is helping us. Aunt Pepsa and I
have tickets to leave on the* Campana. *Rodolfo will wait for his
papers to arrive from Zagreb and follow us in another ship.
Aunt Albina and Uncle Mirko will wait for us there. They were
very happy to know that we are going. I will write to you from
Buenos Aires.*

Mama, we are going so far away! When shall we meet again? I think a lot about what happened to Grandma and Grandpa Banić. God took them away, and I will not see them anymore.

Here I'm sending you a picture of our wedding day, me with Aunt Pepsa. Everyone here calls her Josephine.
Take care. I love you all,
Ángela

Editor's Note: This story entered in the II Family Stories Competition organized in 2015 by Club de Escritura Fuentetaja of Spain.

Faithfulness

"You can stop here, please," Lisa said.

"When will we meet again?" he asked.

"I'll call you soon," she lied.

He smiled at her like moments before when they were in a tight embrace, soaked in sweat and drunk with feverish energy. Lisa would have kissed him again, but she forced herself out of the car and stepped in the sidewalk.

The car left slowly, joining the scarce traffic of early morning. She walked three blocks to an elegant building where the doorman greeted her and let her know that Miss Nina had called the reception twice, asking for her.

Lisa thanked him and went up to see the young woman her husband had hired as an assistant, although Lisa knew it was only to spy on her. When she opened the door, Nina walked to her anxiously, but she did not let her speak. Lisa hugged her with passion, pushed her toward the wall and covered her mouth with an urgent kiss that, like so many times before, erased her absence.

Cinderella
For a Day

With insecure fingers drenched in cold sweat, Joe Restucci rings the bell again. His hand trembles in pain. Damn arthritis. And that woman that never comes when he needs her.

Finally, a young nurse appears at the door, with questioning eyes. Joe looks at her sideways, angrily.

"Well...? Is it time or not?" His voice breaks and he breathes in the oxygen from the tube with difficulty.

"In half an hour," she says with sympathy, which annoys him more still. "You know you have to wait," she adds, and with a professional and neutral gesture helps him to raise his head while removing the pillow soaked wet and replaces it with another from a clean pile on the bed next to his. He accepts in silence, with the helplessness that invades him every time he has to depend on others for the simplest things.

"Hurry up, then! I'm here waiting!" And with a softer tone: "Although I'm not going anywhere..."

He does not want to annoy this nurse too. She is young, but she seems efficient, not like the ones he's had to tolerate before. Joe appreciates efficiency, a quality that he had cultivated all his life and that makes him show little patience with incompetence.

The nurse rinses the small towel in a container of water on the side table and with expert movements cleans the dampness from his forehead, cheeks, and neck. He feels his hair stuck to his skin, those few strands that he has left after the chemo took away his dark and abundant waves from one day to the next.

"I used to have so much hair... that seems unbelievable now," he murmurs almost to himself.

The nurse carefully combs the thin hair, and he feels another wave of fury growing in his chest now almost without air again. Fuck! Why him? This wound hurts so much, and he still has to wait half an hour for the syringe that will calm his pain for a while, that's all. And where the hell is Kitty? She should be here, by his side. He doesn't see her in the room, and his anger grows even deeper inside him. It almost weighs on him like a truck on his chest.

The nurse comes back from the bathroom with fresh water. "Where is my wife?" His voice comes out in a laborious whistle. She gives him a few soft pats, smiling, arranging the oxygen under his nose and stretching the sheet over his chest. He notices the freshness of the fabric on his skin.

"I just crossed her on her way to the cafeteria," she says. "She'll come back in a minute, don't you worry."

The nurse flashes her youthful, white teeth again. Not like his, that at seventy-five already have a dark, yellowish tint, undoubtedly because of the cocktail of drugs that they make him swallow for nothing, after all. If I could, I'd run out of here right now, he thinks, just as a stab of pain stirs his insides again.

Kitty and I were different in every way. But we clicked immediately, as if we had known each other all our lives. "I never thought that the Iron Curtain was going to fall like this, I thought it was forever," she told me, out of nowhere, inside the elevator of the financial company where we both worked as temporary assistants. She was holding the *Cleveland Plain Dealer* with a photo of Reagan on the front page. And right then and there I knew that she was interested in the same things I was. That had not been my experience among the American administrative assistants I had encountered so far.

She was a pretty, freckled redhead, with very short, graying hair, deep green eyes, that fragile skin that results in premature wrinkles and a wide and white smile that appeared for any reason. I was a newcomer, only two years in the country, and spoke English with a strong Hispanic accent.

She was born in a small town in Ohio, and I on the other side of the American continent, but it was as if we had been born only ten miles apart. We were exactly the same age and found we had nearly the same experiences, read practically the same books, danced to the same rock music and enjoyed the changes left by the sixties. It was proof of the influence that at the time the still not baptized "cultural globalization" had had by that time in Latin America.

When we met, she was living with Joseph C. Restucci, an Italian-American millionaire, fifteen years her elder, fervent Roman Catholic and divorced against his will because the ex-wife had left him.

Their relationship began after he hired Kitty as a secretary at his electronic parts manufacturing company. Restucci belonged to The Young Millionaires' Club, a distinction for those fortunate enough to achieve great wealth before the age of thirty. Kitty was a high school teacher, disappointed in her vocation. Soon after they got together, she learned that Joe had an endless feud, as indispensable as an addiction, with his ex-wife. She witnessed scenes worthy of a soap opera, with drama, screams, and door slamming. An eternal crisis that kept him tied to an overpowering woman and two spoiled teenage children who despised him, although he maintained them all in luxury.

His ex-wife sued him often. She accused him of mistreating the children and asked for an increase in alimony. They lived in court from trial to trial and Joe passed her and the boys a hefty monthly payment. The ex-wife was "the other woman" in his relationship with Kitty, who endured the soap opera with stoicism. Between matches of shouting and slamming doors, Joe bought first class tickets and the two of them traveled the world. Festival of Cannes live from a yacht anchored on the coast, a camel ride through the pyramids of Egypt, a climb to the Wall of China, a peek under the iron curtain in St. Petersburg and Prague, a hot air balloon ride over an exotic place, and much more. Kitty found it easy to forget the soap opera episodes with so many brand clothes, casinos, famous people, and international airports. She kept on working as a temp in other companies to maintain some sort of financial independence from him.

Sometime after we met, she confided me that she had convinced him to get married, and he finally accepted. Then, before the wedding, he panicked and disappeared for ten days without a word. She was left waiting in the dark, anxiously juggling all the details of the wedding, not knowing if Joe would appear or not. At last, two days before the big date, he reappeared without explanations, and the magical wedding at a country club in the suburbs was carried out with great success.

Kitty got married wearing her crystal slippers; a pair of transparent shoes, just like Cinderella. I still keep the invitation card to the wedding, printed with silver relief, two rings linked by a bow, with cursive and elegant letters. The motif of the party was *Winter in Wonderland*, and we danced with music from the forties by a big jazz band until very late. Shortly after, she confided to me that she had signed, before witnesses and at the urging of Joe, the sine-qua-non-condition of the wedding: a prenuptial agreement.

The noisy I-hate-you-and-I-love-you between Joe and his ex-wife went on for many years. Eventually, the contact between Kitty and I became more and more infrequent until it was only a greeting card for Christmas.

The nurse leaves the room, and Joe looks at the window. There are shreds of striking white clouds crossing the intense blue skies. His accumulated anger hurts, and because Kitty is not at hand to unburden himself of it, it keeps on growing inside of Joe.

I have worked so hard for others, for Mamma, for my brothers, why doesn't somebody help me get out of this?

Nobody helps me. Where is God? Is there God? Why can't I find peace? I'd bet I'm about to die. That's the only sure thing, but I do not want to, I do not want to die. I do not want this damn pain. Where the hell is my family? They are always at hand when they need money, but... this pain, it hurts so much... And where did Kitty go? And where are those bloodsucking children of mine? I'm sure they're ready for inheritance... but they're not going to give me the pleasure of coming to see me, no. Just like their mother, that witch, Carla, who has not even shown her face here... Why did I marry her? She said she was pregnant, and after the wedding, she announced that she had miscarried... she deceived me well with lies. Mamma did not believe her for a moment, and she was right, Mamma. Carla was looking for a husband to pay for her expensive tastes... Mamma hated her. Ah, but she was beautiful, and she still is... with her robust figure of a woman, not like these skinny females of today... I never wanted to separate from her, that's the truth... divorce is a sin. How could we break something like that? An oath before God! And she went on to marry that insignificant nobody, a teacher. What could have she seen in that bookworm? And to top it off, she went on to have a kid with him... that's why my children became scoundrels, she spoiled them... it is all her fault, as Mamma always said...

The light noise of the door opening startles him, and out of the corner of his eye, he sees Kitty, who enters anxiously and approaches the bed tiptoeing. He tries to return to rhythmic breathing, but each time is harder. And the nurse is not coming yet. She may have forgotten him. They're all the same.

"Are you awake?" Kitty whispers tenderly. "How are you?" "Why are you whispering?" Joe responds abruptly, "no one is sleeping here." Kitty does not flinch. On the contrary, her voice becomes sweeter still. "I can read something to you if that would help you. The nurse will be back in a minute with your painkiller."

He shakes his head, and she lifts a dry towel, dips it in the cold water and cleans his face softly. He closes his eyes, enjoying the freshness of the cloth. Impulsively, Kitty leans over and kisses his parched lips lightly. He opens his eyes and looks at her with something that resembles affection until a flash of pain darkens his gaze.

"It hurts! It hurts so much! Call that nurse once and for all!"

After the injection, Joe struggles to relax, to let the pain be quieted by the potent drug, returning his body to him inch by inch for a while. If only he could breathe easily, without this fatigue. Kitty sits next to the bed with her bestseller book open, ready to get into whatever romantic foolishness she is reading now. It is for the best; he needs silence now.

Sure, Kitty is a good person. She has been with me through a lot... It's not that she doesn't care for my money... although I fixed that with the prenuptial, of course, 'cause family is family. She wanted to marry me at all costs, so she had her wedding. I didn't want to lose her; so I went along with it, although that was not a real wedding like the one with Carla... it wasn't even in a church. We were married by a minister, a woman, for Pete's sake! I went with the flow, it was her dream, and she took care of the whole thing... but one gets married once in life, all else is theater... Kitty needed me, and she was looking for a father figure. I realized that the very first day at that job interview... back in the company... Those were the times...

Something startles him, but Kitty is still there, in silence, reading her love story. Joe closes his eyes again, enjoying the truce that morphine has given him.

Where was I? Oh yes, when Kitty came to the interview, she was so beautiful, fragile and recently divorced from a man who confessed that he was going to live with another guy... What kind of man does those things? I was powerful then, what a time, all achievements and triumphs... To think that those electronic trinkets were going to be used for computers... everything fell right into place, and I was at the top of the world... and all thanks to Mamma. If it were not for her, nothing would have come out that way... What a strong woman she was, how she raised us alone after Pappa had the accident... By sheer willpower and her faith in God... She was better than a father because the old man was lazy, he couldn't keep a job for long. So Mamma always told me how proud of me she was, proud of how I took care of the family... and how everyone enjoyed the comfort and the luxuries that the old man was never able to provide...

With his eyes closed, Joe keeps on thinking about his mother, her moral lessons when he was a teenager full of energy, and how she straightened him out. She was a woman made of steel.

And she was so wise... she was on to Carla early on, that greedy woman fishing for a wealthy husband. I was fifty, a foolish bachelor, so I fell right into her trap. Dear Mamma, she always reproached me how ungrateful I was, abandoning her and the family to get married... but I was by her side until the end, and she forgave me, dear Mamma...

Suddenly Joe is invaded by a strange calm, now nothing hurts, he is floating.

How weird, I feel so light, so well... but what's that, the window seems bigger and brighter... the closer I look at it, the brighter it gets... and that silhouette? Could it be... Mamma?

The beeping, sharp and continuous, startles Kitty, who has been dozing. She jumps out of her chair just as a nurse storms into the room, followed by others. The piercing sound comes out of a black box on the wall that now shows a straight green line that hypnotizes her, and Kitty stares at the light, motionless for a moment, while everyone else fusses noisily around the bed where Joe lies.

"Well, because I thought he was going to leave me the house in his will," Kitty tells me later, from many miles away. Her voice is now more serene, after sobbing for a while on the line. She does not explain which one of the houses she's talking about, but I'm sure it's not the mansion that Joe built in a luxurious cul-de-sac in the suburbs a few years before falling ill. "I fought Carla for the house, and it cost me a lot, but to no avail... I was left with nothing."

Her voice is now calm, casual.

"Kitty," I say, not sure of what to add. "So, where are you living now?"

"In the new house. But it's only until they sell it, then I have to move out."

I do not ask anything else. In fact, I do not really want her to tell me more because I already knew it for years. She goes on, imperturbable. She says that since Joe died a little over a year ago, she has been involved in a long series of legal fights with his ex-wife and children. She presented witnesses and all. I want to ask her, how couldn't you see it coming after Joe made you sign a prenuptial agreement giving up all rights? What could you expect from him? But I can't.

So I change the subject. I ask Kitty about her health, and what keeps her busy now. As if coming out of a trance, she tells me:

"Ah, yeah, I still haven't told you anything about this! It's not good. Just yesterday the specialist gave me the results of some tests I had. It's about that old pain in the abdomen that I used to complain about, remember? Well, it looks like I'll have surgery soon. I have an appointment already. I'll let you know how it goes."

I can barely manage to articulate a couple of questions, my mouth dry and my voice strangled.

"What happened? What do you have?"

"I have a rare form of terminal cancer. The surgery is in a few days, but I hope everything goes well, and the sun will shine again."

I'm speechless. But Kitty has already changed the subject. She tells me about her personal improvement classes and the latest self-help book she has bought.

I listen to her in silence, not knowing that this will be the last time I hear her voice.

In Search of the Missing Pieces

The threads weave themselves idly. For instance, let's take my determination to find a particular character or a setting, or even a topic, and when I reach it, I turn the first idea around and look at it from another angle. No, not this one either, I am not convinced yet, so I better change the perspective again. Ha, from here it seems more interesting, I tell myself, but I am still not there. The days go by, and in the backburner of my mind, this idea is floating around, although not a full project yet, only a few vignettes. Until one day, as we share mate tea and after our daily mutual updates, we start chatting about this and that, and I tell him I am ruminating an idea that still has no shape. So he playfully tosses a couple of funny, loose thoughts, such as: "Well, you could talk, for instance, about *je n'ai plus d'essence*," and I laugh heartedly at the memory of that narrow alley in the financial district of Paris in 1977. Remembering our camper-van out of gas, stuck in the middle of the street, with cars piling up behind us and the French passers-by shouting at me who knows what, while I leaf anxiously through the *Berlitz French For Travelers* to explain my problem. I recall the policeman dressed as Charles De Gaulle, who finally got help to move the van against the curve. And that old lady, an elderly version of Mary Poppins (what would she be doing in Paris, looking so English?), threatening me with her umbrella from the opposite sidewalk. We laugh again at the memories. I picture him, coming back, walking steadily by the middle of the busy street, with a can of fuel in hand, thirty plus years younger, full of energy and, as always, calm and taking things easy. Now he smiles at me and confesses: "I'll never forget the anxiety I felt while buying that fuel. I put some bills in front of the French man of the gas station and told him in English: Here, take it, whatever I owe you, please, hurry." That memory takes us to another, and another. How many adventures we lived on that trip, with the campervan that we rented in London to zigzag through Europe for a few months before settling in a permanent place.

And so the story begins to take shape. I still do not know if this is the one I want to write since it has no form yet, although I know it is there. As an industrious spider forming her web, I weave a section here and another one there, in the air, while we dig into our memories for the anecdotes that we rescue from the many we experienced. The places of the world that we remember among the many in which we set foot; fragments that cannot paint the whole canvas because pieces are missing, although those that I have in mind at this precise moment, these partial images make our eyes shine, trigger smiles and we share a magical moment. We continue with the game, and of course, we draw other not so pleasant memories, like that morning in our apartment in Hawthorne, a suburb of Melbourne, Australia, when I woke up and found myself in a pool of blood. It was the day we lost our first, much-desired pregnancy. Now I have the suffocating lump in the throat that always comes with this painful memory, but he, albeit with sadness in his eyes, imitates Les Luthiers' lyrics, "*Let me go, past, let me go!!*" Those words, as always, snap me out of the bad memories. "Don't forget that on that trip through Europe you were already carrying our baby," he says, always my balance, my emotional axis. "And look what a beautiful daughter she is, the joys that she has given us all these years, on top of that precious granddaughter who greets us on Skype two or three times a week now." I sigh and agree, happy. But we have finished drinking our mate, and the story that I want to write has not taken shape inside me. I still have loose threads. So I grumbling, go to the computer, put my fingers on the keyboard, and look at this Miami garden for some time through the window, and finally say to myself: So what if I do not have a whole story today. I have a lot of loose pieces, and I better put them on paper even if they are just pieces of a puzzle that I can't assemble yet. Some of them seem lost among so many memories, although, if they don't manifest themselves, I know they're floating around. And I'm sure that when I find the exact piece I need, the precise one that will connect all the others, the story will take shape.

Always, as if by magic, it happens.

Editor's Note: Story published on the literary magazine Metaforología.com, on 12/7/2015.

Romance in
Buenos Aires

Patricia strolled down the ten blocks that go from Belgrano Avenue to Tucumán Street. It was Saturday after lunch, and downtown Buenos Aires was getting ready for the weekend by quieting its energetic commercial morning pace. The afternoon siesta calm would last until nightfall when activity would reach its peak. The cafes would fill with customers, and the movie theaters on Lavalle Street and the theaters on Corrientes would be teeming with people in long lines for the next show. The residents of a metropolis that never sleeps would stay up like usual on Saturdays. Except for her.

It had rained early, and Patricia was carrying her umbrella under one arm, just in case, and holding on the other a plastic bag with a neat package inside, carefully wrapped and tied with a light thread.

In a few minutes, Patricia would see Juan José after four long days of waiting. She had put on a new dress and fashionable wide-heeled leather shoes that felt very comfortable. Of course, living in Buenos Aires and walking so much (she hated to take the public buses, always full), her three pairs of shoes had to be modern but very practical. She kept her pair of high heels for special occasions when she could move around by car since the uneven city sidewalks destroyed the fragile heel tips right away.

She hurried down Lima Street, which runs parallel to the broad 9 de Julio Avenue. The wholesale fabric and tapestry stores in the Montserrat neighborhood were closing their doors for the weekend. As she passed by, Patricia peeked at her reflection on an ample window that an employee was about to cover with metal shutters. If the humidity remained high, her shoulder length hair straightened and blow-dried earlier in a tight weave around her head would undoubtedly curl back up in no time.

She shrugged; it didn't matter, after all. Although Juan José preferred her with straight hair, he would love her just the same, she was sure. And now, recovering from the flu, he was waiting for her. Obviously, with him still in bed, the visit was going to be formal... she was expected not to get too close, or kiss him. After he had whispered sweet nothings in her ear on the phone last night, he had clarified:

"As soon as you get here, that bitter old lady will let you into my room, but remember, do not close the door because she doesn't approve of us students receiving women at the house."

"Sure, don't worry, dear, I'll try not to get too close. Are you feeling better now? Did the fever go away?"

"I have a tiny bit of fever still, but I already feel better. Oh, before I forget... bring me the shirts you washed for me. No need to iron, those are wash-and-wear."

"Sure, I'll take them, they're already dry," she had said, happy that he needed her and happy to help him. The thought made her feel a deep tenderness for him. Poor

Juan José. It was so difficult for him to wash his shirts, with the owner of the student's boarding house controlling everything and not letting him hang the shirts to dry outside on the balcony. "Because they can be seen from the street, and we live right downtown and on the second floor," the witch had objected. As if pedestrians walking down the narrow Tucuman Street were ever raise their heads to see to the small patch of sky that can be seen from the sidewalks!

Patricia was lucky in that sense. The owner of the girls' boarding house where she lived, a Galician woman, seldom went to the laundry room, so she did not know if Patricia was scrubbing more clothes than usual by hand. So, after Juan José told her those horror stories, she offered to wash his shirts. There were just four or five per week. It was not so much work after all. It had been a year since she began washing them. Besides, with the meager monthly student's allowance that Juan Jose complained his parents sent him from Salta, he could not afford to take them to get laundered.

Luckily, she managed to get by with the modest salary she earned by typing documents half a day at a legal office, which allowed her to pay for her boarding, buy books and cover other small expenses. Cigarettes were expensive, of course, and she smoked almost a pack a day. But she was doing fine, and Patricia could sometimes foot the bill for both of them at the cheap restaurant where they often dined when Juan Jose had spent all his money. She believed in the equality of the sexes. After all, it was the end of the nineteen sixties, and the world was buzzing with so much remarkable change. University students in Córdoba had confronted the city police and organized the *Cordobazo*, a revolt in the streets that made the military government stagger. In Paris, a whole generation was taking to the streets under the inspired graffiti motto: "We don't know what we want, but we do know what we DON'T want." In the United States, there were marches in the streets against the Vietnam War and in favor of racial equality. And students around the world advised, wisely, to distrust anyone who was over thirty years old.

Patricia devoured the news and read any book that appeared on the subject, while around her, in the boarding house, girls arrived from the provinces looking for work and a formal boyfriend or were about to get married. Didn't they have eyes to see that the world was changing day by day? If Patricia tried to engage them with any talk about the news, they looked at her as if she had just stepped off a flying saucer. It was useless.

Of course, Juan José was not very much in favor of female independence or political changes, either. But that was because he came from a well off traditional family. The old families of the northwest had deep-rooted customs and, indeed, they had instilled in him all that. But, in the long run, she was sure that he was going to absorb the changes, like her. They belonged to the same generation that was making history all over the world, and he was going to receive a law degree in a couple of years, as soon as he passed those subjects that he did not seem to be able to conquer for some time now.

His parents did no allow Juan Jose to hold a job. They wanted him to pass those classes as soon as possible. Patricia helped him with his studies. They sat in cafes for hours before exams, and she reviewed his note cards one by one, again and again with him. So much that she already knew them by heart.

"Who knows, I might go to law school and become a lawyer instead of a journalist." She had teased one night, sipping their third *espresso* coffee while he struggled to remember some historical fact or the number of some law or another.

Juan Jose had given her such a scornful glare that she did not dare to continue with the topic.

"A lawyer, you?" He had snapped back incredulous and with disdain in his eyes. "I do not think so..."

"I'm just joking," she immediately regretted her utterance, and decided not to show what she knew about the subject they were reviewing, so as not to hurt him. Juan Jose had been her life for almost two years, ever since she had finally accepted the first date after he pursued her for months, and she didn't want anything to change.

On Tucumán Street she turned right and walked half a block. While seeking the electric doorbell panel for his floor, Patricia's heart beat faster. Soon she was going to see him again. She had missed him so much while he was bedridden with the flu and he had asked her to stay away for fear of contagion.

The lean, wrinkled woman who greeted her at the door of the floor definitely looked annoyed and stared at her with distrust. Patricia followed her down the dark corridor to a door. When she opened it, Patricia walked into the room where her beloved spent his days studying for the first time.

Juan José was lying on the bed, covered with blankets to his chest, although it was slightly warm in there. The small window that opened onto a narrow gray balcony illuminated the room. She could not take her eyes off his lovely face. The woman glared at them admonishingly as if saying: "you already know the rules," and exited with her head high, leaving the door wide open. Patricia approached him and timidly brushed his hand. He smiled at her.

"Did you bring the shirts, my love?"

"Yes, here they are," she murmured, holding the package without knowing where to put it. Juan Jose pointed to a table against the wall, full of scattered papers and books. She obeyed.

"It is sort of weird to see you like this, in this place," she ventured. "You look pale. Are you sure you really feel better?

"Yes, I'm okay now. Sit down there, in case the old woman passes by, so she won't see you near the bed."

They small-talked for a while. She told him what she had done during the last few days. They also exchanged affectionate words that sounded strange in that place, until finally, she remembered:

"Dear, if you already read *Pride and Prejudice*, I would like to take it back. I offered it to Laura. You have had it for months. But only if you are done with it, of course..."

"To tell you the truth, I could not finish it, it's a bit slow. Those nineteenth-century romances bore me. It must be up there in that pile." He sat up a little. "I'm going to take another aspirin."

"Want me to get it for you?"

"Don't worry. I have them right here. Look around for that book," he said, turning toward the small night table. She stood up, happy to move around, and checked the stacks of books on the three shelves lining up on the wall.

"I don't see it here."

He was busy searching through the drawer of the bedside table for the aspirins, so she kept looking for the book, now on top of the untidy desk. She moved some of the folders and pages until a pile of color photographs suddenly slipped out of a copy of *Automundo Magazine*, half-spilling them onto the other papers. She picked them up and re-grouped them quickly, but as soon as she saw the first one, her heart jumped. Patricia did not have time to think much, because Juan José was already asking with alarm:

"What the heck are you doing, Patricia? Do not touch those papers... what do you have in your hand?"

"A picture of you hugging a blonde girl," she stammered, holding it out for him to see.

He jumped out of bed, dragging the quilt with him, and tried to swipe at the photos, but Patricia leaned back and looked toward the door. He stopped, hesitant, in the middle of the room without knowing whether to go back to bed or chase her at the risk of the owner appearing at any time.

"What the hell is this?" Patricia roared, now understanding what was happening.

"Please don't shout," he begged, going back to bed as if giving up.

"Then answer me! I'm waiting," she said trying to regain control, still cornered to keep her distance. "Explain this to me, please!" Her voice trembled with surprise and anger.

"Sit down. We need to talk."

"You have another woman! You bastard, you have another woman!"

She repeated herself, incredulous, as she quickly reviewed the photos, one after the other. Juan Jose and the girl were in all of them. This beautiful blonde, with incredibly golden long and straight hair, in different poses, with different people, always smiling, always hugging, or kissing. Patricia felt as if she had been emptied from within by a swipe. It was as if she were not there, as if she was suspended in the air, without a body, just eyes to watch the impossible, the unmanageable.

"How could you be such a...?"

"Stop swearing, will you? I don't want people to hear you. Calm down, please! Sit there and stop making a scene!"

She obeyed, like an automaton, because she could not think, her mind was paralyzed.

"You have another woman!" She repeated. Now her voice was calm, the result of understanding the enormity of what was happening.

"It's not another woman," he said, stretching the bed cover, not looking at her face. "She is my fiancé, back home," and when he said it, the sweet northwestern accent of his voice was even more noticeable.

Patricia could not believe what she was hearing, and that's why she stayed there, still, silent, destroyed. Because the gullible side of her expected him to clarify the situation, to explain the misunderstanding, to say no, that what she was seeing with her own eyes was not true, because it seemed unbearable to her.

Juan José kept on talking, mercilessly, without measuring the caliber of the blow he was striking.

"Her name is Maria Soledad. She lives in Chile, I met her several years ago..."

"Keep on talking!"

"She studies domestic economy in Santiago."

"Domestic economy? What type of career is that? Who studies such a thing?"

"Girls who want to get married and take care of their home. Serious girls."

"What...?"

"Look, Patricia, you don't understand, that's why you make fun of people who do not do what you like."

"What the fuck does that have to do with the fact that you have a girlfriend, and you were cheating on me all this time? With you accepting me to pay for your ticket to meet my parents in Rosario, to visit them for the holidays? Were you cheating on her then? And, worst, why do you go out with me at all? Are you going to keep going out with her?"

He looked at her face and now, more in command of the situation, he dared to give her the real blow:

"Maybe it's better that you saw the photos, so I do not have to lie to you anymore."

Patricia was stunned. It took her several seconds to digest what he had just said.

"Lying still more than what you already lied to me?"

He looked at her in silence.

"Answer me!" She ordered.

"Of course, I'm going to stay with her, and I do not *go out with her,* she's my fiancé. I'm sorry you've had to find out this way Patricia because I love you very much. But next week she'll be here with her family to visit Buenos Aires, so we weren't going to be able to see each other for a while. I was about to tell you that I was going on a trip. It's better this way."

She let the information sink in for a few seconds: "See how lucky you are, you won't have to lie like a bastard again. How many times have you lied to me like that, taking me for an idiot?"

At that moment, the owner of the boarding house appeared at the door with questioning eyes, no doubt attracted by the yelling, but said nothing.

Patricia looked around and calmly lifted the package she had brought, opened it, and pulled out the neatly folded shirts.

"What are you doing? Leave those shirts there!"

She glared at him with all the scorn she could muster in her eyes, and without saying a word, she walked to the balcony, opened the door, stepped out, and with a single swing the five wash-and-wear shirts flew out in the wind and rain that by then fell torrentially. Wetting her carefully coifed hair, Patricia leaned over the railing to see them float in the wind and fall in disorder, one on the roof of a public transport bus and two on the sidewalk.

The last two fell on the asphalt of the street, full of water, oil, and soot, to disappear immediately under the wheels of a couple of cars.

She went back into the room, lifted her umbrella and purse and, without listening to the screams of Juan José, enraged, walked by the flabbergasted old woman and went out into the hall.

She could not wait for the elevator, so she run down the stairs, drenched by the rain and now the tears of sorrow that poured down her face without control.

When she reached the street, there was no sign of any shirt, not even those that fell on the sidewalk. Patricia did not open her umbrella. The rain mingled with her tears and she felt her hair curl up completely, freed.

Editor's Note: This story was published in the LAIA III Anthology, *Los Mundos Posibles*, as a finalist in the 2012 International Short Story Competition organized by the Latin American Intercultural Alliance of New York.

Encounter at The Avalon

"It's snowing again," says Julia a bit annoyed although she likes winter.

Since we moved in together, almost a decade ago, she has celebrated every year's first snowfall outdoors with an explosion of energy. However, this time she looks like a caged lion. It may be a remnant of that lingering flu. Or worse, maybe it's because when the years pass, cold weather goes from a stimulating physical boost to a sharp knife that stabs you to the bones.

"Would you like another tea?" I dare to ask, putting my book down on the coffee table near me. She probes around with restless eyes; I can read in her gaze that she is looking for something to do.

"No thanks. Tea already seems to be seeping from all my pores," she mutters, plopping herself among the cushions of the sofa that overlooks the window. She has the dullness that wintertime Sundays invite in this rural Akron suburb, in the middle of nowhere, in central of Ohio.

I try to pick up my book, but she insists, wrapping her legs with the woolen blanket:

"Come on, let's tell each other stories, Beba. Let's recount silly thing we've enjoyed in the past. Nice things.

Anything that takes us out of this gloomy grayness that has engulfed the garden and the town. Maybe one of our trips, I don't know..."

"You want to watch TV?" I always try to dodge down memory lane chats.

"No," she insists. "There are *'seventy-five channels and not one flower,'* like the poem goes. And there are no rental videos left that we haven't already seen."

"Well," I say acquiescent, although with little enthusiasm, "let's think about something."

But I do not want to think. When I dig into our past, I always get hurt by the memories that bombard me from within with no mercy, like splinters stuck under the skin that remain intact on the outside, as if nothing happened. For me, the past has seldom felt better than the present.

"With so much Spanish homework to correct, why don't you work a bit on that?"

"No, Beba, I don't feel like it. I'm almost finished, there are only two or three pages left."

I try to be honest with her:

"Truth is, I can't think of anything nice to remember at this time."

"It doesn't matter," she stands firm adds in a dreamy voice. "Looking at this bare, gray landscape, with the snow that still doesn't stick on the ground, makes me think of Florida. It must be warm down there now. Remember those suffocating Miami summers, our light dresses, looking for a place with air conditioning, walking into any store just to breathe... we were so crazy. Weren't we?"

She doesn't have to say more. Julia always returns to Florida for one reason or another. Why wouldn't she?

There she lived, we lived, our young and carefree years. The '90s were a whirlwind, and it isn't easy to forget them. On the other hand, it is better for me to leave them behind. I also have plenty to remember too, and not everything is pleasant. Like what happened with Josh. When South Beach was an explosion of sculptured bodies in the sun and sex of all kinds.

I look at her face to face, leaving the book on the table again, and out of nowhere I bring up the subject, the subject that I have wanted to talk about for so long, and I never had the nerve to. Well, too bad for her now.

"Tell me again the story of when you met Josh. But tell me everything. No excuses this time, Julia. If you want me to pay attention to you and not return to my book, you tell me everything. With all the details."

I feign strength knowing well that I am asking to be badly stabbed. A voice inside tells me *you're crazy, what are you asking, it's going to be nasty*. But I'm on the way to the abyss now, as I always feel when I think of that. Without blinking, I snap at her:

"Understood?"

Julia measures me with piercing eyes, the same ones she flashes when she knows she's going to hurt me. We know each other inside and out, she and I, as if we were looking in a mirror.

"If that's what you want ... but first, let's have a drink and order a pizza for later. I do not feel like cooking. You don't either, do you?" she says as if calculating how much to hurt me, how far the blade will go. As if measuring the importance of what we have together and if the risk is worth taking.

I return what I think is an indifferent look, while I get up and serve the drinks. If our students saw us now, would they laugh at us? Would they see two pathetic spinsters? They would never suspect the inner fire that still burns inside of us, I'm sure.

She picks up the phone, and I hear her order a pizza, Hawaiian, as always, with little sauce and a lot of cheese. I prepare a salt-free margarita for myself, a whiskey sour for her both on the rocks. Julia is still rearranging the cushions around. In the semi-darkness, she looks like a teenager, with her straight hair falling around her face and her slim body wrapped in flannel pajamas. My stomach tightens by the effort I make to ignore the wave of tenderness that shakes me, right now, when what I need is a nerve.

"Julia, go on... and tell me everything. Now it doesn't matter any more."

"Well, sooner or later it's going to happen," she says, feigning grief, "you can't forget it, can you?"

"No. I won't forget. I just forgave you, but I do remember what happened. Go ahead."

While she shifts around getting ready to talk and sips some whiskey, I wonder why human beings take pleasure in hurting each other. I know I'm still in time to stop it. But, of course, I do not. I want the whole poison at once.

Tell me about when he ordered the drink at the bar. What did you think?'

"Before you came into the bar? You already know that. I've told you the story more than once." I look at her threateningly, and I lift up my book. She hurries. "Okay, okay. I was waiting for you at the bar. That day the Ávalon was full of tourists. I got to the hotel's lobby, and you were not there yet, so I ordered a drink, scanning the place. That's when I saw him coming out of the elevator." She hesitates for a few seconds, but her imploring eyes do not inspire pity in me.

"All. Everything you thought."

"Well, he walked to the bar and asked for something, without looking around. I was sitting in one of the sofas, and I don't know what happened to me. I swear I've never experienced something like it. I started to tremble. I had to put my glass on the table as my hand was shaking so much. Josh was so beautiful, tanned, with that white shirt half unbuttoned his hair highlighted by the sun, his dark green eyes... " Julia looks at me, and I glare back impatiently. She continues: "I could not take my eyes off him, and finally, he saw me. Beba, I swear it was my fault; he had to notice my inviting stare... He picked up his beer from the bar and approached me slowly, smiling deliberately, as if he knew me."

She is silent now, lost in the gray of the window that is reflected on her eyes in the form of shadows. Julia knows I do not like beating around the bushes, so she turns to look at me.

"Why didn't you come down to the bar at the time we agreed?" she says reproachfully.

"Do not digress, please," I cut her short.

She sighs, and after another sip, she goes on, talking almost without breathing:

"I was hot for him. It was at first sight. I would have grabbed him right there, right behind the counter if I could have. My skin was burning, my heart galloping. We could not stop looking at each other; it was an electric current that crossed for an eternity between the two of us. Finally, he introduced himself. I do not know what he said or how I didn't melt right on the spot. We talked for a few minutes, but I don't remember what we said. I was mystified by his accent until I found out that he was French-Canadian. He pulled a hotel card from his wallet, wrote a number on the back and handed it to me. I took it, like an automaton, still unable to take my eyes from his smiling lips." She pauses for breath. "And right at that moment, you came into the bar."

After so many years, jealousy still feasts on me like a vulture. Julia continues, with a pleading voice now:

"How was I supposed to know that he was the guy who was going out with you? When I saw him at the bar, I thought it was one of those splendid gay men that swarmed around the hotel and the beach, one more handsome than the other. That's why it took me by surprise when he approached me that way."

"It doesn't matter. Do not make excuses. Go on with the story. Don't get side-tracked."

"So, after you got there, remember, the three of us had dinner, and then you both took me to my hotel."

"Precisely!" I cut in with bitterness. Now I can't hide it, I want to let it all go to hell, I want to clarify things with her and finally get this thorn out of me. "That's why after you found out he was mine you called him, you still went to bed with him, didn't you? So now you will tell me all the details, everything. Because he confessed it to me and I will know if you're lying. Go ahead!"

"Beba, how can you say that? If you won't believe me, why do you want me to talk?"

"Just tell me everything," and I prepare myself for the punch I'm asking for.

"Well, I called him the next day. That night I couldn't sleep, thinking about him, about you, about you two together. Full of guilt, I had restless dreams... The next day we met after he left you at the hotel. You went to sleep, exhausted from the day of sailing, remember?"

I move my head nodding. Sure, I remember. I remember the tryst he and I had down in the sailboat's cabin. I was in heaven. He murmured so many sweet things in my ear. And all the time he was thinking of his date with her.

"Where did you meet? And where did you do it, if you can tell me?"

"He took me to a friend's duplex," she said. "I did not ask anything. To be discreet, we met at The Penguin's bar, which is, as you know, quite far from the Ávalon. I walked there like in a dream. He took me by the hand, and we waited for the car at the door. I told you I was going to the movies with Marcela. I almost ran over the valet boy, I was so nervous trying not to be seen." She sips again from her drink, without looking at me. "Josh got into the car, and his aftershave hypnotized me. He put his hand on the gearshift, but he picked it up, and with his hand covering mine he managed to change gears. Every time we stopped at a light, his warm fingers caressed me softly up my arm, driving me wild. We did not say a word. Sometimes I looked at him out of the corner of my eye, his neck smooth, his jaw straight ... I felt so aroused, but also guilt burning in my chest," she says, with downcast eyes. Julia does not dare to face me.

"Well, I'm waiting."

"Never before did such a thing happen to me." Her voice quivers. "When we got to the building, he parked, and we went up to the duplex. I was in the clouds. In the elevator, he lifted my hair back with his hands and kissed the back of my neck. Then I looked at him. We kissed feverishly, with a desperation that I cannot explain." She pauses. I do not say anything. I just shake my head, indicating she should continue, but I raise my glass and take a long drink. My throat is as dry as cardboard.

She also takes a sip of whiskey.

"He was anxious, like me... He could hardly put the key in the lock. Finally, we entered. The apartment was dark, the only light coming in from the street through the curtains. Josh closed the door after I entered and right there, without letting me take another step, he leaned me against the wall of the little hall and began to undress me slowly, gently, silently and kissing me all over." She pauses again and looks at me. She has the eyes of a deer in headlights.

"Keep on going," I say without mercy and wanting to jump at her neck and yell at her face how much her words are hurting me.

"What, everything?" There is disbelief in her voice.

"You guys did it, didn't you? Well, now put it in words..." I do not finish the sentence that I have on the tip of my tongue: *so that you can see yourself doing the vile thing you did to me.* I cannot even speak.

She drinks some of her already watered whiskey with difficulty, and continues, in spite of herself:

"You know how Josh was... full of passion and tenderness at the same time. We went to a sofa in the living room, and I began to undress him the way he had done with me. He had such a beautiful skin I wanted to kiss it and not stop..." Julia's vice trails and her eyes get lost in the window with the memory of his body, of that skin that I knew inch by inch and that I had tasted with my own lips repeatedly.

I feel that I hate her with all my being and I cannot erase the image of the two of them on that sofa. Deadly jealousy stifles me. How can I continue living near this woman? Why don't I push her out of my life?

"Tell everything once and for all!" I almost shout at her. She hurries now, her voice breaking:

"For when he... well, I was almost finished. But he continued caressing me. He made me finish several times... nobody had ever made me feel that way. In heaven and in hell at the same time."

"Did you reach orgasm together?" I jump, fearful.

"No," she says piously, and I want to believe her.

Julia covers her face with her hands, and now I notice the tears running down her face.

"After that, we left the apartment," she sobs. I wait. Then she continues, now lost in her memories: "We kissed desperately through the empty corridor and then in the elevator, knowing that it was a farewell, feeling guilt but no regrets, neither of us. And that's it." She shakes her head. "Honestly, that was it."

Now she fixes her swollen and reddened eyes on mine. I am full of rancor, accumulated for years and I am trying to finally release it from inside me so that it doesn't hurt me anymore. I have no words left, nor do I want her to say more.

I go to a bookshelf and take out a brown leather album of photos, almost faded by the years and by the urgent hands that had opened it thousands of times. I look for the page, and I find it. I approach Julia with the album open. She knows what photos are there and her eyes are questioning me.

"Look again," I say, calmly now, pointing to a blow-up of Josh that takes the entire page. He is sitting at one of the Ávalon tables, next to the railing on the sidewalk of Ocean Drive. His shirt is half open on his tan chest, his green eyes sparkling and those teeth, incredibly white against his sensual lips.

Julia looks at him tenderly.

"This is the last one you took, right? A couple of months after that day..." she says with a sad smile, now without fear. "I remember so well, it was a few hours before the accident. He was so beautiful."

"Yes. Josh was beautiful in every way. Maybe it was his mix of English, Italian and French, who knows. But I always felt that he was not entirely mine, that he was like a fleeting ray of sunshine." I say with longing, although I feel idiotic. Now the memory of him and his sudden, useless death disarms me entirely again.

Julia looks at me.

"You're right, Beba, he was like a passing ray of sun, and we were lucky that he struck us both."

The silence that follows is heavy with contradictory feelings. It is a shared silence of reproaches and forgiveness, of memories and nostalgia. For the first time, the luminous vitality of Josh unites us, instead of separates us. I set the album carefully on the little side and sit next to Julia. The snow that falls outside is more defined now, the flakes whiter and thicker. She remains quiet beside me, hesitant, like me.

After a moment and in a mutual impulse, we embrace each other tightly, feeling connected as we had never felt before.

ISABEL GARCÍA CINTAS was born in Córdoba, Argentina, studied journalism and photography in Buenos Aires and lived for three years in Melbourne, Australia. On her return, she settled in San Carlos de Bariloche, in the Patagonian region of southern Argentina, where she worked in radio and the written press. Isabel moved with her family to the United States in 1987.

She has published two novels: **Incident in Patagonia (Incidente en la Patagonia**, Spanish edition), a suspense story that deals with the theme of the thirty thousand disappeared civilians during the military rule of the 1970s, and **Del Mediterráneo al Plata** (in Spanish), a family saga based on the emigration of her grandparents from Italy and Spain to Argentina. Her last book is **The Old House and Other Short Stories (La Casa Vieja y Otros Relatos**, Spanish edition).

Some of her short stories appear in three anthologies: **Poets and Narrators of 2012**, by the Institute of Peruvian Culture of Miami, **Los Mundos Posibles**, by the Latin American Intercultural Alliance of New York of the same year, and **Primera Antología Cáncer de Mama**, published in 2015 by Talento Comunicación Editorial of Spain. She is a staff member of the digital cultural magazine *Letra Urbana*.

Isabel lives with her husband in South Florida since 2001.

Author's Website: www.isabelgarciacintas.com

OTHER BOOKS FROM THE AUTHOR

INCIDENT IN PATAGONIA - English Edition
INCIDENTE EN LA PATAGONIA- Spanish Edition

Awarded Suspense or Mystery Honorable
Mention at the 2015 Latino Into Movies
Awards organized by Latino Literacy Now,
Los Angeles, CA   http://www.lbff.us

Along the lines of The Secret in Their Eyes
(2009), and The Official Story (1985),
this page-turner touches a contemporary
and ever pressing subject: The
consequences of an authoritarian and
repressive
government taking over a country.

**Two old Argentine friends meet in Brooklyn,
New York for dinner. A manuscript from a
woman that has just died in jail exchanges
hands with the request for it to be published.**

A gripping political thriller by Award Winner Isabel Garcia Cintas set in
the beautiful city of Bariloche, Argentina, during the military rule years,
1976-83. The protagonist, a young journalist, works under strict media
censorship. One evening she is intercepted and warned by suspected
secret services men. Later on, when Susana, her colleague and best
friend from childhood is kidnapped in Buenos Aires, she decides to
search for her. The ensuing odyssey to find her friend will change her
life forever.

Amancay Ediciones – 309 pg.
Available at Amazon and Barnes & Noble websites
www.isabelgarciacintas.com

DEL MEDITERRANEO AL PLATA
Historias de Familias
(Spanish Edition)

A family saga based on the memories of the author's Italian and Spanish grandparents and great-grandparents. A novel that spans from the late nineteenth century to the mid-twentieth century.

Compelling stories of courageous men an women who traveled by boat from the Mediterranean Sea to La Plata River in search of a better future. At a time when distances were immense, communications scarce and, to the majority of the emigrants, return to the native country would become an impossible dream.

Amancay Ediciones – 525 págs.
Available at Amazon and Barnes & Noble websites
www.isabelgarciacintas.com

www.ingramcontent.com/pod-product-compliance
Lightning Source LLC
Chambersburg PA
CBHW022153260626
47155CB00017B/1864